Evie looke
in h...

The man above her blotted out the sun. Evie could tell immediately that he and the girl she'd just met were related. But Faith's eyes were still warm with laughter. The man's were as chilly as the water lapping at her toes.

"I'm Evie McBride." She scrambled to her feet to retain her dignity. "Your daughter and I bumped into each other."

Sam looked from the slender redhead to his niece in disbelief. He'd been looking for Faith for the past hour—so he could ground her for the rest of her life. He hadn't expected to find her in the company of the uptight schoolteacher his dad had warned him about.

But somehow his father had forgotten to mention that Evie McBride was a *beautiful* uptight schoolteacher....

KATHRYN SPRINGER

is a lifelong Wisconsin resident. Growing up in a newspaper family, she spent long hours as a child plunking out stories on her mother's typewriter and hasn't stopped writing since! She loves to write inspirational romance because it allows her to combine her faith in God with her love of a happy ending.

A Treasure Worth Keeping
Kathryn Springer

Steeple
Hill®

Published by Steeple Hill Books™

STEEPLE HILL BOOKS

Steeple
Hill®

ISBN-13: 978-0-373-81350-6
ISBN-10:   0-373-81350-3

A TREASURE WORTH KEEPING

www.SteepleHill.com

Printed in U.S.A.

But store up for yourselves treasures in heaven, where moth and rust do not destroy, and where thieves do not break in and steal. For where your treasure is, there your heart will be also.

—*Matthew* 6: 20–21

To Linda—
A fellow traveler on the writer's journey.
I'm glad we're in this together, friend!

Prologue

"**P**lease think about it, Evie. You're the only one of us who doesn't have—"

At the sound of a meaningful cough, Caitlin's words snapped off and Evie McBride smiled wryly.

Who doesn't have a life.

That's what Caitlin had been about to say before Meghan, "Miss Tactful," had broken into the conversation. They were talking on a three-way call, the usual method her two older sisters used to gang up on her. Sometimes advanced technology made life easier, and sometimes it was simply a pain in the neck.

"What Caitlin was going to say," Meghan continued in an annoyingly cheerful voice, "is that you're the only one whose summer schedule is…flexible."

Flexible. Nonexistent. Was there a difference? And if Evie had known how many times she'd be called upon to be *flexible* over the past few years since their father had retired, she wouldn't have chosen teaching as a career. She would have tied up her life with a neat little job that kept her working year-round, like her sisters had.

It wasn't that she minded helping out their dad. They were extremely close and she loved him to pieces. No, what drove her crazy was that Caitlin and Meghan always assumed she didn't have any plans for her summer vacation. And that just wasn't true. A neat stack of novels, the ones she hadn't had a chance to read during the school year, sat on the floor beside her bed. There was a miniature greenhouse in her backyard full of tomato seedlings waiting to be nurtured. And a gallon of paint in the hall closet, ready to transform her front door from boring beige to Tuscan yellow because she'd read somewhere that a front door should sport a friendly, welcoming color. And really, was there anything more friendly than yellow? Evie didn't think so.

"What if I have plans?" Evie asked. The sibling ambush had occurred at nine o'clock at night, interrupting her favorite educational program. There had to be some consequences for that. Unfortunately, stalling was all she could come up with.

"You do?" Meghan asked cautiously.

"What plans?" Caitlin demanded.

Now she was stuck. "Painting."

"Painting." Caitlin repeated the word like she'd

never heard of the activity, and Evie could picture her rolling her baby blues at the ceiling.

"Is it something you can put off for a few weeks, Evie? Once I'm done with this photo shoot, I'll try to take some time off to help you." Meghan, bless her heart, let her keep her dignity.

Silence. Evie's cue to cave in. After all, that was her role. She sighed into the phone, knowing her sisters would accept it as the cowardly white flag of surrender that it was.

"All right. Fine. I can run Beach Glass while Dad goes on his fishing trip."

"Dad will be so happy." Caitlin's voice was as sweet as glucose syrup now that she'd gotten her way.

Evie resisted the urge to stick out her tongue at Caitlin's smiling face in the family photo on the coffee table.

"Evie, we *really* appreciate this," Meghan said. "And Dad will be thrilled. He didn't want to have to close up the store for two weeks."

"But he didn't want to ask you for help because he didn't want to take advantage of your free time," Caitlin added.

"Well, it's a good thing *you* don't have a problem with that, then, isn't it?" Evie said.

But not out loud.

What she said out loud was *good night,* allowing just a touch of weariness to creep into her voice. Hopefully enough to generate a smidgeon of guilt in her sisters' consciences. Not that it would matter when another crisis barked at the trunk of the McBride family tree. Why these crises always surfaced during the months of June, July and August, Evie didn't know.

Three years ago, Patrick McBride had officially retired from teaching and bought a small antique shop, whimsically christened Beach Glass by the previous owner. A quaint stone building, it sat comfortably on the edge of a lightly traveled road that wound along the Lake Superior shoreline. A *very* lightly traveled road. It wasn't even paved. The first time Evie saw it, she had a strong hunch why the previous owners had practically *given* it away. They'd probably cashed the meager check in nearby Cooper's Landing on their way out of town, anxious to rejoin civilization.

Evie had spent most of that summer making the year-round cottage that had been included in the deal suitable for her father to live in. The calluses still hadn't completely disappeared.

The following summer she'd been the one drafted to spend "a few days" teaching their dad how to use a computer so he could manage all the financial records for the business. The brief computer lesson had turned into a month-long project that had ended with Patrick's mastering of the power button and not a whole lot more.

The previous summer, Caitlin's tail had gotten tied

in a knot when Patrick happened to mention a woman's name *twice* during their weekly phone conversation. A Sophie Graham. Evie had flatly refused to act as the family spy. Her dad was an adult and it wasn't any of their business if he'd found a friend. Less than twenty-four hours after Evie had drawn a line in the sand over that situation, Caitlin had figured out a way to tug her over it. Beach Glass needed to be landscaped and since the only thing she and Meghan knew about plants was that the root part went into the ground, Evie was the obvious choice to spend six weeks mulching and planting flower beds.

Suspiciously, her sisters were always too busy to help out but never too busy to call and check up on her.

But Evie loved them. Even bossy, tell-it-like-it-is Caitlin. And she knew they loved her. And really, was it their fault all she could find to fill up three months of summer vacation was painting her front door, transplanting tomato plants and living vicariously through the lives of the characters in her favorite books?

Evie had missed most of her program during the kissing-up portion of the conversation so she turned off the television and closed her eyes.

I want my own story, God.

Even as the thought rushed through her mind, she treated it like the mutiny that it was.

Your own story! What are you talking about? You're a junior high science teacher. Shaping impressionable minds. It's a high calling.

Wasn't she the first teacher who'd taken the Rock of Ages Christian School to first place in the science fair competition the past few years? While all the other schools had entered working volcanoes and posters labeling the parts of a rocket, her students had brought in *inventions*. Like Micah Swivel's solar-powered toaster. And everyone knew the reason Angie Colson won the spelling bee with the word *bioluminescence* was because Evie had just finished a unit on insects. The day before, Angie had taken the chapter test and had chosen fireflies, a stellar example of bioluminescence, as the subject of her required essay. They'd shared the victory, celebrating with doughnuts and hot chocolate in the teachers' lounge.

Evie basked in the knowledge she had been loved by every seventh and eighth grader in her charge since the school had hired her. And if their test grades didn't prove their devotion, the number of cookies on her desk every morning did.

She had a story all right. It just happened to be woven into the lives of an age group most people ran, screaming, away from. She thrived between the months of August and May. The summer months made her feel restless. And lonely.

Maybe that's why she didn't fuss too much when her sisters rearranged her summer plans. It was nice to be needed. And she couldn't deny that their father, whom they affectionately referred to as the absent-minded professor, needed a watchful eye.

Evie reached for the phone and pressed Speed Dial.

"Hello?"

"Hi, Dad. I hear you're going fishing."

Chapter One

Sam Cutter had driven almost twelve hours when an old joke suddenly came back to him. Something about a town not being the end of the world but you could see it from there.

Now he knew that place had a name. Cooper's Landing. And it was cold. No one had warned him that winter released its grip with excruciating slowness along Lake Superior's shore. The second week of June and the buds on the trees had barely unfurled in shy, pale shades of green.

He drove slowly down the main street and pulled over next to the building that sagged tiredly on the corner. The color of the original paint on the clapboard siding was only a memory, and the shingles had loosened from the roof, curling up at the ends like the sole of a worn-out shoe. A red neon sign winked garishly in the window. Bait.

He glanced at the girl slumped against the window in the passenger seat. Her lips were moving silently, showing signs that yes, there was brain activity. Since she hadn't talked to him for the past five hours, he'd been forced to watch for obvious signs of life. They'd been few and far between. Changing the song on her iPod. The occasional piece of candy being unwrapped. A twitch of her bare toes. Well, not completely bare. One of them had a toe ring.

He touched her elbow and she flinched. Sam tried not to flinch back. Once upon a time she'd been generous with her hugs.

"Faith? I'll be right back."

She frowned and yanked out a headphone. "What?"

"We're here. I'll be right back."

She straightened, and her gaze moved from window to window. She had a front-row seat to view Cooper's Landing, and Sam expected to see some expression on her face. Shock? Terror? Instead, she shrugged and pushed the headphone back in place.

He wished he could disengage from reality and disappear into another world so easily.

The warped door of the bait shop swung open when he pushed on it, releasing an avalanche of smells. The prominent ones were fish, sauerkraut and bratwurst. Sam's eyes began to water.

"Let me guess. Cutter. You look just like your old man."

Sam saw a movement in the corner of the room

just after he heard the voice. Between the heavy canvas awning shading the street side of the building and the tiny row of windows, the sunlight couldn't infiltrate the inside of the bait store. Shadows had taken over, settling into the maze of shelves. The lightbulbs flickering over his head held all the power of a votive candle.

"Sam Cutter." Sam walked toward the voice.

He heard a faint scraping noise and a man shuffled toward him out of the gloom, wiping his hands on a faded handkerchief. By the time he reached Sam, he'd stuffed it in the pocket of his coveralls and stretched out his hand.

"Rudy Dawes."

Sam shook his hand even as he silently acknowledged that a long, hot shower and half a bottle of the cologne he'd gotten for his birthday weren't going to completely strip away the bait store's unique blend of odors.

"I wasn't expecting to see you so soon. S'pose you're anxious to get a look at her." Rudy squinted up at him.

"That's why I'm here."

Rudy started to laugh but quickly broke into a dry, hacking cough. "Come on, she's outside."

Sam followed him to the back of the store, and his boot slipped on something, almost sending him into a skid that would have taken out a shelf full of fishing reels. He didn't bother to look down, not wanting to know what was filling the tread of his hiking boot. In some cases, ignorance *was* bliss.

Rudy pushed the door open, and Sam found himself standing on a rickety platform that trembled above an outcropping of rocks. At the base of the rocks, a blackened, water-stained dock stretched over the water. With one boat tied to it. Sam stared at it in disbelief as it nodded in rhythm with the waves.

"There she is. The *Natalie*. She's a beauty, ain't she?" Rudy tucked his hands in his pockets and bowed his head in respect against the crisp breeze that swept in to greet them.

"*That's* the boat?"

Faith had materialized behind them, and Sam twisted around to look at her. She'd pushed her chin into the opening of her black hooded sweatshirt but the tip of her nose was pink, kissed by the wind.

"It can't be." Sam blinked, just to be sure the faded gray boat wasn't a hallucination due to the sleepless nights he'd been having. "When I talked to Dad, he said the boat was *new*."

"He's one of them positive thinkers." Rudy grinned and spit over the side of the railing. "It was new to him when he bought it. I can tell your first mate here knows quality when she sees it."

Faith's shy smile reminded Sam of his manners.

"I'm sorry, Mr. Dawes, this is my niece, Faith Cutter. Faith, this is Mr. Dawes."

"Aw, it's just plain Rudy." He smiled at Faith, revealing a gold-capped front tooth. "Jacob said you wouldn't be here until mid-July. And he shoulda warned you we don't pack away our winter coats until then."

Sam glanced at Faith and noticed she was shivering. Instinctively, he wrapped his arm around her shoulders and pulled her into the warmth of his flannel-lined denim jacket. Instead of pulling away, as he half expected her to, she tunneled in farther. For a split second, she was six years old again, snuggled up against him with a copy of Dr. Seuss's *One Fish, Two Fish* book in one hand and a raggedy stuffed rabbit named Mr. Carrots in the other.

"Dad said the boat was available whenever I wanted to use it," Sam said distractedly. "June... worked out better for us."

"Doesn't matter to me none. I just keep an eye on it for him. Go on now. Get acquainted with her."

Faith skipped down the skeletal wooden staircase that spiraled to the water. Sam was tempted to yell at her to slow down and grab the railing, but one look at it made his back teeth snap together. It was probably safer *not* to use it.

By the time Sam hopped on board, Faith had already disappeared below deck. From his dad's description of the boat, Sam thought he'd be in a luxury cabin cruiser for the next few weeks. Now he simply hoped it was watertight.

"Sam!" Faith's muffled voice sounded more excited than it had in months. "You've got to see this!"

He ducked into the narrow stairwell and found her standing in the doorway of one of the cabins.

"Can I take this one?"

Sam peered in cautiously. A narrow bunk bed, a corner desk and a small table were the only furnishings in it, but even though they were old, everything was spotless. He exhaled slowly in relief.

"Sure. The desk will come in handy."

Faith rolled her eyes in typical twelve-year-old fashion. "You had to remind me."

"That was the deal. Your mom let you come with me if you kept up with your homework."

"Mom would have let me come anyway." Faith lifted her chin defiantly, but he could hear the tremor in her voice. "I heard her. She told you that I've been 'too much' for her lately."

Sam closed his eyes. He had no idea that Faith had overheard his last conversation with Rachel. "Faith, it's not you. Your mom… Things have been hard for her the past few months."

"Well, here's a news flash." Faith's eyes narrowed and suddenly she looked years older. "Things haven't been easy for me, either…."

Her voice choked on the word and Sam pulled her against him. He wasn't sure what he could say to comfort her. Not when he hadn't discovered anything to fill in the fissures in his own heart.

"I miss him." Faith clung to him.

The knot of sadness forming in Sam's throat strained for release, but he kept a tight rein on it.

"I miss him, too."

"I thought you were only staying two weeks, Evangeline."

Evie saw the mischievous gleam in her dad's eyes and handed him another duffel bag from the trunk of her car. Patrick was the only person who called her by her full name, a gift from her parents to her paternal grandmother, the first Evangeline McBride, when she was born. "A person can't be *too* prepared."

"But what is it you're preparing for, sweetheart? A tidal wave? Or maybe an asteroid?" Patrick peered in the car window at the flats of tomato plants lined up across the backseat.

Evie was used to her dad's teasing. "Don't be silly." She handed him a large sewing basket embroidered with strawberries. And a stadium umbrella. "We'd have plenty of time to get ready if one of those things was going to occur. This stuff is just for…every day."

Her dad frowned as she handed him a bag of groceries. "There *is* a grocery store in Cooper's Landing."

"Do I need to mention that the expiration date on the can of corn I bought last summer coincided with the Reagan administration?"

Patrick winked at her. "You love it here."

He was right, but Evie wasn't about to admit that to Caitlin and Meghan.

A week after school had officially closed for summer vacation she'd packed up her car, locked up the house and driven away with her traveling companions—the box of books on the passenger seat beside her.

The closer she'd gotten to the adorable stone cottage her dad now called home, the more excited she'd been. When Patrick left on his fishing trip, Evie knew she'd be perfectly content just to stretch out on the wicker chaise lounge in the backyard and admire the lake from a distance. She loved watching Lake Superior change from steel-gray to vivid blue, depending on its mood. And Superior was a moody lake. The proof was in the hundreds of ships that slept below her ice-cold surface.

Evie leaned close and kissed her dad's bristly cheek. "You forgot to shave again this morning."

"I didn't forget," Patrick grumbled. "I'm retired. A man shouldn't have to shave when he's retired."

Evie looped the strap of a canvas messenger bag over her shoulder and headed toward the house. "Did you and your friend finally decide when you're leaving?"

"Day after tomorrow. Jacob's picking me up at five in the morning. And—" Patrick put up his hand to prevent her from saying what he knew was going to come next "—you don't have to get up and make oatmeal for me. The reason we're leaving so early is because it's a long drive to the lodge, and then we have to get to our campsite."

"Why don't you just stay at the lodge?" They'd had this conversation several times already, but Evie thought it worth repeating. Until she got her way. Patrick was only fifty-nine, but she didn't understand why he'd turned down a soft bed in the main lodge for a tent on a secluded island several miles away.

"Jacob's been camping for years," Patrick said. "He'll take care of me."

Evie snorted. "From what you've told me about Jacob Cutter, he's a daredevil. I don't want him to talk you into anything stupid. Or dangerous."

"You've been teaching the peer-pressure curriculum again, haven't you?"

Evie gave a weak laugh. "I'm sorry, Dad, it's just that I want you to be careful."

"Careful is my middle name."

"Stubborn is your middle name," she muttered under her breath.

The sound of tires crunching over gravel drew their attention to the vehicle creeping up the long driveway.

"Looks like you've got some customers," Evie said, watching a black pickup truck rattle into view.

"Maybe they're lost." Patrick grinned. "But I'll still try to talk them into buying a pair of seagull salt-and-pepper shakers."

Evie laughed. Beach Glass didn't have a single

kitschy item like the ones he'd just described. Her dad spent the winter months combing estate sales to find rare objects—the ones that escorted his customers down memory lane. Patrick had told her more than once that everyone needed a connecting point to their past. Sometimes it was a book they remembered reading as a child or the exact twin of the pitcher their grandmother had used to pour maple syrup on their pancakes when they were growing up. Beach Glass was off the beaten path, but people still managed to find it. And when they left, it was usually as the owner of some small treasure.

"Just put that stuff by the door, Dad, and I'll take care of it in a few minutes." Evie couldn't help glancing over her shoulder at the truck idling in the tiny parking lot next to the antique shop. The tinted windows obscured the inside cab from view. She hesitated a moment but whoever was driving the pickup wasn't in a hurry to get out.

She went inside and finished unpacking her clothes, glad she'd tossed in a few sweaters. A person could never be too prepared and the breeze off the lake still had a bite.

When she peeked outside half an hour later, the truck was gone. She poured two iced coffees and headed across the yard to the shop. More than half the furnishings in her own home were compliments of Beach Glass, and she was eager to see the latest bounty her father had added since her last visit.

"What do you mean he's staying on the boat?"

Evie paused at the sound of Patrick's agitated voice through the screen door.

"Well, that's just one of our problems...." His voice lowered, ebbing away like the tide, and then strengthened again. "He stopped by a little while ago, insisting we bring him along. No, I don't trust him any more than you do, Jacob...but Sophie—"

Evie realized she was holding her breath. She'd never heard her dad sound so stressed.

"I suppose we can delay the trip but I'm afraid if we don't go as planned, Sophie is going to get... No, go ahead. Evie might be on her way over. I'll talk to you later this evening."

It suddenly occurred to Evie that she was eavesdropping. She backed away from the door, replaying the part of the conversation she'd overheard.

The elusive Sophie Graham again.

Evie had never seen the woman, even during the reconnaissance mission Caitlin had tried to set up the previous summer. In the interest of maintaining sibling harmony, Evie *had* dropped a few subtle hints to her dad that she'd like to meet Sophie sometime, but all she could get out of him was that the mysterious Sophie wasn't in good health.

"Evie?"

She froze midstep.

Her dad may have been a bit forgetful but apparently there was nothing wrong with his hearing.

Evie winced and caught her lower lip between her teeth. All the times she'd preached to her students that honesty was the best policy came rushing back. She pressed the glasses against her cheeks to put out the fire in them. The downside of having red hair and fair skin. She couldn't hide a blush to save her life.

"I brought you a reward for working so hard," she called through the screen door.

Patrick appeared on the other side and Evie could see the furrows in his forehead, as deep as stress cracks in a wall.

"So, did you sell some of those salt shakers?" Evie asked, deliberately keeping her voice cheerful to cover up the guilt nipping at her conscience.

Patrick's mouth tightened. "No. He wasn't interested in buying anything."

"Who—"

"Let's take this out to the garden, shall we? You can enjoy the fruit of last summer's labor while you take a break. Some of the plants are already coming up, and it's going to be beautiful."

Evie handed him one of the glasses and saw his fingers tremble as he reached for it. Worry scoured the lining of her stomach.

"Dad, is everything all right?" She tried to piece together the fragments of the conversation she'd overheard. It had sounded like someone else wanted to come along on the fishing trip. But why would that upset him? And what did Sophie Graham have to do with it?

"Right as rain."

"There's nothing right about rain unless you have an umbrella," Evie said promptly. It was an old joke between them, and she relaxed when he smiled.

Maybe her concern over the fishing trip was making her read more into the conversation she'd overheard. It was possible her father was simply a little uptight because he was taking a vacation for the first time in—Evie did a quick calculation—twelve years. Not since the year her mother was killed.

Chapter Two

Evie had her alarm set for five-thirty. Not to make sure Patrick ate his oatmeal but to make sure he didn't forget anything. Else.

She pulled on her robe and slipped into the kitchen, only to discover her sneaky father had already left. The coffee was on and he'd left a note taped to the refrigerator.

I'll call you as soon as I can. Relax. Love, Dad.

Evie snatched the note off the fridge and frowned. The faint smell of bacon and eggs lingered in the air. No wonder he hadn't wanted her to get up before he left. He'd wanted to eat his artery-clogging breakfast without a witness.

And what exactly did he mean by *relax*? Was she supposed to relax because she was on summer vacation? Or was she supposed to relax while knowing her dad, who thought one pair of socks per day was sufficient, was going on a two-week fishing trip with Jacob Cutter? A former Marine. The two men had known each other only six months, and already Jacob was pushing Patrick out of his familiar routine. Evie didn't like Jacob Cutter. Her dad was a scholar, not an outdoorsman. A retired high school English teacher. What was Jacob thinking?

Her doubts about the trip had increased the evening before while Patrick packed his things. Evie had noticed an important piece of equipment missing from the gear piled by the door. When she'd called his attention to it, Patrick had laughed self-consciously and disappeared outside to rummage around in one of the outbuildings, finally returning with a fishing pole.

Shortly after watching her dad hook his thumb on one of the lures, Evie had had a burst of inspiration. She could go with them. As the cook. Keeper of the campfire. That sort of thing. When she'd brought it up to Patrick, he'd looked less than enthusiastic. In fact, he'd looked slightly offended and had reminded her that the reservations were for *two* people and they couldn't add someone else this late in the game. Which meant the owner of the black pickup truck who'd tried to coerce Patrick and Jacob into taking him along wasn't going, either.

No wonder Patrick had run out on her so early in

the morning. Maybe he'd thought she'd stow away in the backseat.

Too bad she hadn't thought of that sooner.

If only her dad would have mentioned the fishing trip to *her* before he'd brought it up to Caitlin and Meghan, who'd both thought it was a great idea. Of course. They always had their passports ready to go at a moment's notice.

"Dad never does anything." Meghan had listened to her concerns and gently brushed them aside. "He loves to go to auctions and estate sales and putter in the store, but maybe he's decided he needs to expand his interests. You know, find a new hobby."

Caitlin, as usual, had been more direct. "Don't be such a worrywart, Evie. Dad wants to go fishing, not skydiving. If you see a parachute in the trunk of his car instead of a fishing pole, call me."

It was easy for her sisters to live their own lives and let their dad live his. Both of them had already moved away from home when Laura McBride had died unexpectedly. Meghan had been a freshman in an out-of-state college, and Caitlin a graduate student in France for a semester abroad. Evie had just turned fourteen and she'd been the only one left to take care of Patrick.

Lord, you'll take care of Dad, won't you? Keep him safe and comfortable, just like I would if I were with him? Don't let that reckless Jacob Cutter try to talk him into doing anything dangerous. And help him remember to change his socks if they get wet.

Patrick had always encouraged her to talk to God, her heavenly Father, as easily and naturally as she talked to him. Some people might think she was crazy to talk to God about wet socks, but Evie figured if God knew when a sparrow fell to the ground, He cared about the details of His children's lives, too. No matter how small.

She opened her eyes, ready to start the day right. Beach Glass officially opened at ten o'clock, giving her time to weed the garden and go into town to pick up a gallon of milk and some eggs.

She'd just make sure to check the expiration date before she bought them.

Cooper's Landing was five miles from the antique shop, yet Patrick thought nothing of hopping on a rickety old bicycle and riding it into town. Evie kicked the tire with her toe, and when it wobbled back and forth like a toddler taking those first precious steps, she decided to drive her car instead.

Johnson's Market stuck to the basics—not bothering to cater to the tourists who used Cooper's Landing as a brief resting point to fill up their vehicles and stretch their legs a bit.

The sandy stretch of beach, strewn with sculptures of satin-smooth driftwood, drew Evie's attention when she stepped outside the store with her purchases. Ever since Patrick had moved to what Caitlin referred to as "the end of nowhere," Evie had been fascinated by Lake Superior. She'd grown up in a suburb of Milwaukee, where the only connection she'd had with water was the local swimming pool. But here, right in front of her eyes, the lake stretched across the horizon in variegated shades of blue. And even though today the water was a comforting shade of indigo, it could change with a turn of the wind.

A glance at her watch told her there was time for a short walk down to the dock. She tucked her groceries into the backseat of her car and headed toward the water. Picking her way down the rocky bank, Evie vaulted over a small ledge of rock and practically fell on top of someone.

"Hey!" A girl rose up from a crouched position. "What do you think you're... Oh, sorry."

"I'm the one who's sorry," Evie apologized. "I was staring at the water and didn't see you."

"That's okay." The words came out grudgingly.

She looked to be in the same age range as Evie's students, so Evie knew better than to take the edge in her tone personally. The girl hugged a sketchbook against her chest, and a metal case on the ground by her feet revealed a rainbow of oil pastels.

"You're drawing the lake? Or the boat?"

"The lake. The boat's kind of ugly."

Evie couldn't argue with that. The boat tied to the dock was as plain and drab as a cardboard box. And looked about as seaworthy.

"I admire anyone with artistic ability." Evie held out her hand. "Evangeline McBride. Science geek."

The girl's eyes met hers shyly and then she smiled. "My name's Faith. I'm a jock."

"What sport?"

Faith shrugged. "You name it."

"But Lake Superior inspired you, huh?"

"No, I'm being forced. It's art class." Faith peeked at the sketch pad and made a face. "It's terrible."

Evie knew better than to push. If Faith wanted her to take a look at her drawing, it had to be her idea.

"Okay. Tell me the truth." Faith suddenly flipped it over for Evie to see.

"It's…" Evie's voice trailed off when she saw the gleam of humor in Faith's eyes. She'd colored the entire page blue. "You captured it perfectly, I'd say. A closeup of the water."

"*Very* close up!"

Faith giggled and Evie joined in.

"Faith!"

The voice behind them startled Evie. Her foot slipped on the rocks, sending an avalanche of stones skipping down the bank.

"Hi, Sam." Faith's giggle changed to a bored monotone.

Evie looked up and sucked in her breath. The man looming above them blotted out the sun. Evie could tell immediately that he and the girl were related. Both of them had silver-gray eyes and thick, shadow-dark hair. Faith's eyes were still warm with laughter, but the other pair trained on Evie were as chilly as the water.

"I'm Evie McBride." She scrambled to her feet to regain her dignity, but it didn't matter. She barely reached the man's broad shoulders. "Your daughter and I sort of…bumped…into each other."

Sam looked from the slender redhead to his niece in disbelief. He'd been looking for Faith for the past hour—so he could ground her for the rest of her life. He was pretty sure he had the authority. Although Faith might not agree. The truth was, they hadn't been agreeing about much the past few days, and Sam was at the end of his rope. Moodiness he could cope with, but Faith had started to disappear whenever the opportunity presented itself. Like an hour ago.

They'd been staying with Jacob, who'd left early that morning on a fishing trip, and Sam had brought Faith into town with him while he got the *Natalie* ready to launch. This would be the first time they'd had an opportunity to take the boat out. While he'd checked the engine, his wily niece had pulled another disappearing act.

He hadn't expected to find her in the company of Patrick McBride's daughter. The uptight schoolteacher his dad had warned him about. But somehow Jacob had forgotten to mention that Evie McBride was a *beautiful* uptight schoolteacher.

And he hadn't expected to hear Faith giggling the way twelve-year-old girls were supposed to giggle. The sound had thrown him off balance. He realized he hadn't seen Faith smile or heard her laugh for a long time. Too long. Dan's accident had been like a scalpel—going in deep and removing the laughter from all of them.

"I'm Sam Cutter—"

"He's my uncle, not my dad," Faith interrupted.

Sam exhaled silently. No one knew better than he did that he couldn't fill Dan's shoes. His twin brother had been a great dad, and all Sam could be was what he'd always been—a doting uncle. But lately he found himself wondering if that was enough to keep Faith from drowning in grief. When Dan had been injured, she'd taken a leave of absence from school. Now she was so far behind, the principal had said the only way she could pass to the next grade level was by completing her homework over the summer. What bothered Sam the most was that Faith didn't seem to care.

"Cutter? Are you related to Jacob Cutter?"

"I'm his son." Sam noticed the instant change in Evie's expression.

"It's nice to meet you."

Sure it was. Jacob hadn't been kidding. Evie McBride *didn't* approve of him. He wondered why. "Dad mentioned you're minding the store while he and Patrick are fishing."

"I don't know a lot about antiques, but I do know how to dust them." She glanced down at Faith and winked.

Faith grinned back.

Maybe Ms. McBride came across as a little stuffy, but she definitely had a way with kids.

"Faith, are you ready? We should be long gone by now." Sam stared his niece down, not ready to let her off the hook for disappearing on him.

Faith shifted uncomfortably and he saw a flash of good old-fashioned guilt in her eyes. *Good.*

"Are you house-sitting for your dad?" Evie directed the question at him, her voice polite but strained.

Sam suppressed a smile. With that tone, she sounded just like a prim schoolteacher. All she needed was a pair of horn-rimmed glasses and a bun. They'd go really well with the heavy cardigan she had buttoned up to her chin and the ankle-length denim skirt.

"We're staying on the *Natalie*." Faith pointed to the boat nodding drowsily in the waves.

"You're living on *that?*"

Sam bristled at what sounded like an accusation. It scraped against the doubts he was already having about bringing Faith along. So the *Natalie* wasn't the best-looking boat in the harbor. And maybe she didn't have all the latest bells and whistles. But he'd checked her over, and she was sturdy. The engine had purred like a kitten before settling into a reliable, even hum.

"A few days on the water and a few days at the cabin." Sam lifted one eyebrow, daring her to comment.

Evie McBride's chin lifted, accepting his challenge. "I don't think—"

"You should come with us sometime," Faith broke in, leaving both adults momentarily speechless.

"That's sweet of you, Faith, but…" Evie turned and stared, almost mesmerized, at the water. "Beach Glass is going to keep me pretty busy over the next few weeks."

She was afraid of the water, Sam realized in surprise. His gaze dropped to the hem of her skirt, where the toes of a sensible pair of shoes peeked out. Not exactly the type of footwear designed for splashing in the surf. He hid another smile.

"I should get going, too. The shop opens at ten." Evie's expression softened when she looked at Faith. "Be careful when you're out on the lake."

Sam expected Faith to give Evie her signature don't-fuss-over-me-I'm-not-a-little-kid-anymore look, but his niece nodded solemnly.

"Sam knows what he's doing."

Sam's mouth dropped open at the confidence he heard in her voice. Before he had a chance to bask in the glow, she skipped down the rocks toward the dock. "I can't keep up with her."

He realized he'd said the words out loud when he felt Evie touch his arm. The warmth of her fingers soaked into his skin. When he glanced down at her, he saw a knowing look in her eyes.

"Don't try to keep up with her." Evie smiled. A genuine smile that sparkled like sunlight dancing on the water and had a curious effect on his pulse. For the first time, he noticed a dusting of cinnamon freckles on her nose. "The secret is to stay one step *ahead* of her."

On the way back to the cottage, Evie couldn't stop thinking about Faith Cutter. *And Sam.* Although she didn't want to think about him. Anyone who would take a child out in a boat on a lake as unpredictable as Superior for any length of time had to be a live-on-the-edge type of person. And in the end, that kind of person always hurt the ones closest to them, whether they meant to or not.

Just like her mother.

Growing up, Evie had loved hearing the story of her parents' romantic courtship. Her father and mother had met in the principal's office of the local high school. Patrick had been a first-year English teacher and Laura McIntyre—*Officer* Laura McIntyre—had been invited to talk to the students for career day. The principal had asked Patrick to give Laura a tour of the school before the assembly started.

They'd married six months later.

Growing up, Evie had been blissfully unaware of the dangers of her mother's career. By the time Evie was in middle school, Laura had been promoted to sergeant and spent the bulk of her time at a desk, scheduling shifts and taking complaints.

And then one day, Laura hadn't come home on time. Evie could still see the look on her father's face when the squad car pulled into the driveway and the chief of police had walked up to the front door.

Laura had been struck and killed by a drunk driver while assisting a stranded motorist.

Patrick's strong faith had never wavered, and he'd appealed to his daughters to lean on God, not blame Him for Laura's death. But in the following months as her family handled their grief in different ways, Evie had struggled with a growing realization. It wasn't God she was angry with. It was her mother, for choosing a career that had put her at risk.

Chapter Three

Evie's first customers of the day turned out to be newlyweds who spent more time exchanging loving glances than they did browsing through the aisles.

She felt a stab of envy as she watched the young man press a lingering kiss to his bride's cheek. The young woman, who didn't look much older than Evie, blushed and halfheartedly pushed him away. Evie pretended she hadn't seen the kiss. There were times she asked God why He was waiting so long to bring her future mate into her life. She liked to think God was working on a certain man's heart, making sure he was just right for her so when they met, she'd recognize him at a glance....

Sam Cutter's face flashed in her mind, and Evie fumbled the ironstone pitcher she'd been dusting. Fortunately, she caught it again before it hit the ground. *Sam Cutter!* Not likely. He wasn't exactly

Mr. Personable. In fact, she'd sensed he'd found her…amusing. She hadn't missed his quick, appraising glance when she'd stood up. Or the half smile on his face when his silver gaze had lingered on her wool cardigan. It *was* chilly by the shore. Not everyone had an internal thermostat that made them comfortable wearing a T-shirt on a cool day.

Which brought to mind the tanned, muscular arms his T-shirt had revealed…

"Ah, Miss?"

The bride's tentative question zapped her back to reality. *Snap out of it, Evie.*

"I'm sorry. Can I help you?"

"We'll take this." She pushed a small figurine toward Evie. A ceramic horse with one ear missing.

"Did you notice it's chipped?" Evie wanted to make sure Patrick's customers were satisfied with their purchases when they left.

The woman nodded. "I don't care. It looks just like the horse I had when I was ten. And believe it or not, half her ear was missing, too."

Her husband hovered nearby while Evie carefully wrapped the figurine in tissue paper.

"Enjoy your trip," she called after them.

The store remained quiet for the rest of the afternoon, so Evie took advantage of the time by rearranging shelves and washing the leaded-glass windows in the store.

Solitude was wonderful during the day when she

could see boats out on the water and the glint of the church steeple as it winked back at the sun. But as the sun melted into the horizon and shadows began to sift through the trees and creep toward the door, Evie realized it wasn't so friendly at night. To counteract the silence, she turned on her dad's ancient record player and curled up in a chair with one of the books she'd been waiting since Christmas to read.

It was just after eight when the motion lights in the front yard came on. Evie walked over to the window and peered outside. All she could see was the outline of a shadowy figure walking up the sidewalk toward the house.

Evie's breath caught in her throat until she saw the person's face briefly illuminated in the light.

Sam Cutter.

She hurried to open the door. His clothing looked rumpled from a day out on the water, and his hair was in disarray, combed by the wind. She didn't understand why he'd come for a visit so late in the evening, unless...

"Is Dad okay? Did you hear something?"

"I imagine they're fine. I haven't heard otherwise."

Relief poured through Evie. "Then why—"

"I'm sorry. I didn't realize you'd be tucked in for the night already." The faint smile had returned.

Evie didn't like his choice of words. He made it sound as if she were a chipmunk, hiding in a hole.

"Come in." Evie stepped to the side and he stalked

past her. Her traitorous nose twitched at the pleasing scent of sunshine, wind and sand that clung to his clothes. "Where's Faith?"

"I didn't leave her alone on the boat, if that's what you're thinking."

That *had* been what she was thinking, and the warmth flooding into her cheeks gave her away. Evie ducked her head so he wouldn't notice.

"My father mentioned that you're a teacher, Miss McBride."

"Evie," she corrected, wondering where this was going. "That's right. I teach seventh- and eighth-grade science classes at a Christian school—"

"Faith needs a tutor."

The terse interruption reminded Evie of Caitlin. Her back stiffened like an irritated cat.

"A tutor." Evie repeated the words, giving herself a few extra seconds to process the unexpected statement. Was Sam simply stating a fact or asking *her* to be Faith's tutor?

"We're planning to stay in Cooper's Landing for…a while," Sam said. "We'll be out on the water most of the day, but in the evening we'll be back at the cabin. Faith needs to finish some of her classes before school starts in the fall and someone has to check her progress. Are you interested?"

Sam didn't bother to fill in the gaps. Originally, he'd planned to come to Cooper's Landing alone, but when Rachel, his sister-in-law, had found out, she'd insisted a change of scenery would be good for Faith. Sam had agreed reluctantly, not because he didn't love spending time with Faith but because he couldn't find a way through his own mixed emotions. How could he help Faith deal with something he wasn't dealing with very well himself? And then there was Faith herself. The happy-go-lucky little girl he'd spoiled since the day she was born had turned into a sullen stranger.

When Faith had laughed with Evie that morning, it had made Sam realize just how much his sweet-tempered niece had changed over the past few months. Maybe she needed someone outside the family to motivate her to get her schoolwork done. A tutor. And Evangeline McBride—with her funny wool cardigan and disapproving eyes—happened to be the perfect solution. She obviously liked kids or she wouldn't be a teacher. And maybe a woman would be able to navigate Faith's changing moods better than he could.

"I don't know." Evie perched on the edge of a leather chair and stared at him. "What exactly does Faith need help with? Did she fail a class?"

Sam walked to the window and stared outside at the darkness. "Not yet. She got…behind…a few months ago and didn't have enough time to make up the work she missed. Rachel, Faith's mother, talked to the principal and he said if she completed the work over the summer she could move on with the rest of her class."

Evie sensed there was more to the story than what he was telling her. Questions tumbled over each other in her mind. Obviously, since Faith's last name was Cutter, her mother, Rachel, must be Sam's sister-in-law. But Sam hadn't mentioned his brother—Faith's father. Several things didn't add up. If Faith needed to catch up on her schoolwork, why was she vacationing on a boat with her uncle instead of working on her classes at home with her parents? Maybe Rachel and Sam's brother had divorced.

The possibility softened Evie's initial reservations. Losing a parent under any circumstances was traumatic, especially for someone in an already vulnerable age group like Faith.

"I'll only be here for two weeks," Evie reminded him. "And I have the shop to take care of."

Sam turned to face her again. "We'll work around your schedule. What time do you close for the day?"

"Four o'clock."

Patrick lived on his pension, so Beach Glass provided a supplemental income and gave him the luxury of flexible hours. He could open the antique shop late and close early, even take a day or two off if he felt like it. And her dad had encouraged Evie to do the same if necessary.

"I don't expect you to do this out of the goodness of your heart," Sam said. "I'm willing to pay you whatever you think is fair."

Evie wasn't sure why he put her on the defensive.

She was usually a very easygoing person. "It isn't about the money."

"Then what *is* it about?" He crossed his arms.

If he could be blunt, so could she. "Why can't *you* help her?"

Sam's jaw worked, and for a moment Evie didn't think he was going to answer. He thrust his hands into the front pockets of his faded blue jeans. "She… I don't think she wants anything to do with me." It was clear the admission stung.

Evie remembered the change in Faith's tone when Sam had joined them on the beach. Faith was at the age when she was beginning to assert her independence—to try to figure out just who Faith Cutter was and how she fit into the world.

Evie knew from experience the "tweenage" years had a tendency to put unsuspecting parents into a tailspin. Especially parents who weren't expecting the radical change in their homes when formerly cheerful, compliant kids entered the hormone zone. And if there'd been some kind of upheaval in Faith's life, the fallout could be even worse.

"She's been taking off a lot lately." Sam must have read the expression on her face because he quickly amended the statement. "She's not at risk as a runaway. Eventually she comes back. She either wants attention or time alone. I'm still trying to figure that out. But today—when she was with you—it was the first time I've heard her laugh in months."

Evie's heart, which had a soft spot for kids Faith's age anyway, melted into a gooey puddle. She remembered the glimmer of humor in Faith's eyes when she'd shown Evie her drawing of Lake Superior. Maybe she'd gone through a difficult time recently, but the faint spark of life—of laughter— hadn't been extinguished. It just needed tending. Evie gave in. Not because Sam needed her but because *Faith* did.

Okay, Lord, I'm going to assume this opportunity is from you. But did you have to include Sam Cutter?

"How about two hours a day? After I close up the shop in the afternoon?"

"We'll make it work."

"I thought you were going to live on the boat for a few days at a time."

"You'll only be here two weeks, but we'll probably be here longer. There'll be plenty of chances to take the boat out."

Even though Evie had agreed to tutor Faith, she needed to cover one more base. The one that would give her a clue whether or not the next two weeks were going to be a battleground. "How does Faith feel about this? Does she know you're here?"

Silence.

Uh-oh. Evie's eyebrow lifted.

"She knows I'm here," Sam finally admitted. "She didn't seem very happy about it but then she said, and I quote, 'Whatever.'"

"That's because it was your idea. The 'Whatever' meant she's not totally against it. Which makes my job easier." Evie hid a smile at the uncertain look on Sam's face. Obviously, he had no insight into the workings of an adolescent girl's mind.

As if his internal defense radar picked up on her smile, the uncertainty in Sam's eyes faded and it was back to the business at hand. Evie wondered briefly what Sam did for a living. Even in worn blue jeans and a faded black T-shirt, he oozed confidence. She could easily imagine him in an expensive suit, making important decisions in a high-rise office building, miles above the cubicle crowd.

Sam glanced at his watch. "Can you start tomorrow? We can hammer out more of the details then. Faith is spending the evening with a friend, and I promised I wouldn't be late picking her up. Sophie's one of those peculiar people who go to bed early."

Evie ignored the unspoken words *just like you* that hung in the air between them. "Sophie Graham?"

"That's right. You know her?"

"I've never met her, but Dad has…mentioned… her once in a while."

"Sophie's place is just down the road from us. Her dog had a litter of puppies a few months ago, and that's where I usually find Faith if she's missing."

Which gave Evie the opportunity she'd been hoping for. "If you give me directions, I'll come over to your place tomorrow."

"Are you sure? I don't mind driving Faith over here."

"I'm sure." Evie didn't hesitate. Maybe to break the ice between her and Faith, they'd take a walk down the road to see those puppies. And she'd finally get the opportunity to meet Sophie Graham.

Sam waited until he heard the lock on the front door click into place before he strode back to his car.

The antique shop really was off the beaten path.

He paused, scanning the trees that formed a thick wall between Evie McBride and civilization. Her closest neighbor was two miles away. As cautious as she seemed to be, he was surprised she didn't have any trepidation about staying alone on a secluded piece of property. Not that Cooper's Landing was a hotbed of criminal activity, but with the tourist season starting, the place drew a lot of people from outside the area.

None of your business what Evie McBride thinks or doesn't think, Cutter.

All that mattered was that she'd agreed to be Faith's tutor for the next two weeks.

Faith met him at the front door of Sophie's home, a drowsy puppy cradled in her arms.

"Sophie is going to let me name this one," she whispered, her eyes sparkling with excitement.

Sophie appeared in the doorway behind his niece. She was close to his father's age but still a striking woman, her beauty enhanced by the kind of smile that lit her up from the inside out. "I hope you don't mind, Sam. That puppy is Faith's favorite, so I thought it was only right that she be the one to name him."

"I don't mind." Sam was about to reach out and ruffle Faith's hair but caught himself. The last time he'd done that, she'd shrieked and disappeared into the bathroom, emerging only after she'd washed, blow-dried and styled her hair all over again. Later that day, they'd climbed to the top of an observation deck at Miner's Castle, where the wind had given her a new hairdo that made her look as if she'd been caught in a blender. She'd laughed. Go figure.

"I can't think of a good name," Faith fretted, rubbing the puppy's silky ear.

"Give him one to live up to," Sophie suggested, resting one hand on Faith's shoulder. "How did it go with Patrick's daughter? Did she agree to it?"

"Yes." Sam didn't bother to mention the split second when it had looked as though Evie would refuse to help Faith. The split second after he'd mentioned money. She'd looked offended he'd even brought up the subject, and he wasn't sure why. He didn't expect her to give up her time for free. "She's coming over tomorrow afternoon."

"Why don't you come in for a few minutes. Faith and I made cookies and we're just finishing up the last batch."

Sophie looked so hopeful that Sam didn't have the heart to say no. She ushered them into a small living room where the sparse furnishings looked old but well cared for. His gaze zeroed in on the man sitting at a desk in the corner, hunched over a computer keyboard.

Jacob had mentioned that Sophie had a son she didn't talk about very often. And now Sam had a hunch as to why.

"Tyson, would you like something to eat?"

Tyson looked up and scowled. His thin face was streaked with acne scars. Strands of dishwater-blond hair had been pulled back into a ponytail that trailed between his shoulder blades. "I told you I'm not hungry, Mom."

"You're going to ruin your eyes staring at that screen all night," Sophie scolded lightly. "At least turn around so I can introduce you to Sam Cutter, Jacob's son."

"Hey." Tyson barely glanced at Sam.

Sam saw the hurt look on Sophie's face before she murmured an excuse and disappeared into the kitchen. Faith followed her, still cuddling the puppy.

"That's a pretty nice setup you've got," Sam said, moving closer to see what Tyson was so focused on. He found himself staring at a blank screen. Tyson had shut down whatever program he'd been working on. A red flag rose in Sam's mind, especially when he noticed Tyson's shoulders set in a tense line.

"Thanks." Tyson's eyes glittered with resentment at the disruption. He yanked a pack of cigarettes out of his shirt pocket and shook one loose from the package.

"Outside with those, Ty." Sophie returned with a plate of cookies in one hand and a pitcher of milk in the other. "You agreed not to smoke in the house."

Tyson shoved the chair away from the desk and stalked out of the room.

"I'm sorry." Pain shadowed Sophie's eyes. "Tyson just lost his job last week, so he had to move back home while he looks for another one. He just got here this morning."

Sam didn't consider losing your job an excuse to be rude, but he didn't want to say so. Sophie looked embarrassed enough. "Those cookies smell delicious. How many am I allowed to have?"

Sophie brightened. "As many as you want. I miss feeding hungry men now that Patrick and Jacob are gone. I hate to say this, but Tyson is a picky eater."

Judging from Tyson's bloodshot eyes and sunken cheeks, Sam had a strong hunch the guy preferred to drink his meals.

He took a cookie from the plate Sophie offered and hid a smile when Faith reluctantly put the puppy on the floor. With her skinned knees and her mussed-up hair, she looked twelve years old again instead of twenty. Spending the evening with Sophie had been good for her.

"Faith and Evie will get along well." Sophie smiled at Faith as she handed her a glass of milk. "I feel like I know her already. Patrick brags about those girls of his constantly. Evie was voted Teacher of the

Year last fall in their school district. According to Patrick, it was the first time a teacher at a Christian school won the award. From what Patrick says, out of the three girls he and Evie are the most alike."

Sam remembered the cardigan. *Poor guy.*

"Maybe he was referring to their adventurous streak."

Wait a second. He must have missed something. *Evie McBride? Adventurous?* Sam tried not to laugh. "I doubt it, Sophie."

And as far as Sam was concerned, a guided fishing trip at a cushy lodge didn't qualify as adventurous in his book.

"The whole trip was Patrick's idea," Sophie went on. "I only pray that Bruce Mullins can help them."

Mullins. The name sounded familiar. "Is Mullins their fishing guide?"

"He is a guide there, but he's not taking them fishing."

She'd completely lost him. "But that's why they went to the lodge. To go fishing."

"Oh, dear." Sophie bit her lip and set her glass down on the worn coffee table. "Is that what they told you?"

Every nerve ending in Sam's body sprang to attention at the odd inflection in her voice. "Dad said they were going on a two-week fishing trip at a place called Robust Lodge, which caters to retired businessmen."

"They'll probably do some fishing," she said weakly.

Sam took a deep breath. Judging from Sophie's expression, she was trying to figure out a way to explain without incriminating the two men.

"Sophie, it's all right. What's going on?"

"The whole trip is for me," she finally said. "Bruce is an old friend of your dad's, and they need his help."

"His help?"

"To find the treasure."

Chapter Four

From the roof of the cabin, Sam watched Evie get out of her car. He pushed to his feet, anchoring the hammer into a loop in the toolbelt around his waist. He didn't have time to retrieve the T-shirt he'd discarded earlier in the afternoon. It lay in a damp heap near the base of the chimney, just out of reach.

Evie lifted her hands to her hair, tucking in a few strands that had dared to escape from the sedate braid. Her slender frame stiffened as Jacob's flock of guinea hens charged around the cabin to greet her. The birds were as tame as dogs but as noisy as a squadron of fighter planes.

Sam expected her to dash back to the safety of her car. To his astonishment, a smile tilted the corners of her lips as the guinea hens swarmed around her feet, looking for a treat. Jacob always kept a handful of corn kernels in his pockets, a ritual Sam hadn't realized

Faith had started to copy until he'd found a layer of soggy corn in the bottom of the washing machine.

Sam yanked the handkerchief out of his back pocket and swiped it across his forehead.

What was he supposed to tell her?

He wasn't sure Evie would take the news very well that instead of fishing, their fathers had somehow gotten involved in a wild-goose chase to find a sunken treasure.

Evie took a few steps toward the cabin and spotted him on the roof. She stopped dead in her tracks, shading her eyes against the sun with her hand as she looked up at him.

"Isn't that dangerous?"

Now he was positive she wouldn't take the news well. Not if standing on the roof of a one-story building was her idea of dangerous.

Thanks for leaving me to clean up the mess, Dad.

After hearing stories about how overprotective Evie was when it came to her father, Sam could understand why Patrick hadn't told her the truth behind the trip. According to Jacob, Evie had even driven up to Cooper's Landing the previous summer, apparently suspicious of Patrick's friendship with Sophie. No wonder the poor guy had moved to Michigan's Upper Peninsula to escape her coddling.

Keeping Evie in the dark made sense, but what Sam couldn't figure out was why *his* father hadn't confided in *him*. But he had a strong hunch it had something to do with Dan's injury. As a carpenter, Jacob had spent the majority of his life after the Marines fixing things. Until he had come up against two things he couldn't fix. His wife's illness and…Dan. Now Jacob had been presented with an opportunity to help a friend and feel useful again.

Sam couldn't blame his father. Jacob coped with his feelings of helplessness one way and he had chosen another.

The conversation with Sophie the night before had been quite enlightening. And frustrating. Sam had spent half the night battling his conscience. Evie had generously agreed to help him by tutoring Faith. Didn't he owe her the truth? But if Patrick didn't want Evie to know what he was up to, was it his place to fill her in? And it wasn't as if there was any cause to worry. Jacob and Patrick were grown men, certainly capable of making their own decisions without getting flack from their adult children.

Sam had no doubt the men could handle themselves. It was adding Sophie to the mix that made the situation more difficult.

Her story wasn't his to share. She hadn't been able to provide many details because Tyson had slunk back into the living room, abruptly ending the conversation. It was obvious Sophie didn't want her son to overhear them. From the brief conversation, however, Sam had managed to put together a few of the pieces.

Sophie had been working on her family's genealogy when she was diagnosed with cancer. While searching through family archives, Sophie discovered diaries kept by her grandmother that exposed a skeleton in the Graham family closet. A scandal caused when a ship sank in Lake Superior and her great-grandfather, Matthew Graham, apparently saved himself and a young woman's dowry. No one else had survived.

At that point, Tyson interrupted them and Sophie had quickly changed the subject.

Sam buried a sigh and dodged between the boxes of shingles scattered on the roof, pausing long enough to scoop up his shirt. By the time he reached the ladder, Evie stood below him, holding the bottom of it.

"They do make aluminum ladders nowadays, you know," she called up to him. "They don't rot. They're splinter free. And they're equipped with multiple safety features."

Sam suppressed a smile. *You've got to be kidding me.* "I'll keep that in mind."

Sam bypassed the last three rungs of the ladder and landed on his feet beside her, light as a cat.

Evie averted her gaze as he pulled the damp T-shirt over his head and rolled it down over his abdomen. As if he knew exactly why she'd looked away, his eyebrow lifted in a silent question.

Better?

He was laughing at her again. Heat coursed into Evie's cheeks and she took a step away from him, knowing her freckles had lit up like laser dots against her skin. She took a deep breath and decided to focus on the reason she was there.

"Is Faith inside?"

"I think so. She was helping me but took a break about an hour ago."

The glint in his eyes told Evie he was deliberately baiting her. She took the bait anyway.

"I don't think that's a good idea—"

The guinea hens drowned her out as they recognized Sam's voice and charged. He sank his hand into the pocket of his tattered blue jeans and retrieved a fistful of corn, tossing it on the gravel.

"*Numida meleagris,*" Evie said without thinking.

Sam pushed his hand down his leg to wipe off the dust and looked at her. "What?"

"*Numida meleagris.* The Latin name for guinea fowl."

"I'll take your word for that, Miss McBride." Sam scraped a hand through his hair and ended up tousling it even more. "I should probably warn you. Faith doesn't really like science. Or math."

"She enjoys English? History?"

Sam shook his head and a few strands of dark hair flopped across his forehead. Evie resisted the urge to smooth them back into place.

"Gym class."

"She's into sports." Evie remembered that Faith had described herself as a jock the day they'd met on the beach. That didn't bother her. In a school like the one she taught in, the smaller ratio of students to teachers allowed her to focus on each individual child. Over the years, she'd found creative ways to tap into her students' natural abilities to make learning more fun.

"Don't get me wrong, she's a good student," Sam told her. "But she'd rather study basketball plays than sit down with a textbook."

"Is there anything else I should know?"

A strange expression flickered across Sam's face, but he shook his head. "I can't think of anything."

"Good, because I hate surprises."

Sam glanced at the canvas bag looped over her shoulder. "Here. Let me carry your...suitcase? You didn't have to bring your own books, you know. Faith's mother sent up an entire library."

"I've got it. And, just to set the record straight, it's a purse, not a suitcase."

"What do you have in that thing?"

"Oh, the usual stuff."

He studied the bulging bag. "Sleeping bag? Jumper cables? The kitchen sink?"

Evie saw the look on his face. "Of course not. Just the essentials." Her laptop computer. A miniature sewing kit. Tape measure. Collapsible umbrella.

"You must have been a Girl Scout."

Her eyes narrowed. Was he mocking her? "It's always good to be prepared."

The cabin door flew open, and Faith stepped onto the narrow porch. Evie guessed the reason behind the mutinous look on the young girl's face. Even though the two of them had connected over Faith's sketch of Lake Superior, Evie's role had changed. Instead of a kindred spirit, now she was the person responsible for making sure Faith kept her nose buried in the books.

Evie almost laughed. It wouldn't take long to put those fears to rest. "Hi, Faith."

"Hi." Faith studied her toes, refusing to meet Evie's eyes.

"Did you get your books out like I told you to?" Sam asked.

Faith shot him a look ripe with resentment. "Yes."

"Faith? Remember what we talked about this morning."

Judging from the edge in Sam's voice and the anger simmering in Faith's eyes, Evie doubted they'd talked at all. She guessed Sam had lectured and Faith had tuned him out.

"We don't need any books today," Evie said. "We're going on a field trip."

Sam and Faith both turned to stare at her.

"A field trip?" Sam sounded skeptical.

"For science class. We're going to study *Canis familiaris.*"

"Good. Great." Sam looked way too eager to escape. "I'm going back on the roof. I'll see you later."

"Sam?" Evie dug in her bag and pulled out a plastic bottle. "Here. Sunblock. The sun isn't as strong this late in the day, but you should still wear it. Or, ah, your shirt. That would work, too."

You aren't only a geek, Evie, you are officially their queen.

Sam stared at the bottle as if it were a live grenade and then at her. Evie braced herself, expecting to see amusement lurking in his eyes. She was used to it. Over the years her sisters had developed entire stand-up comedy routines based on her cautious ways.

We're not laughing at you, Evie. We're laughing with you.

To her amazement, Sam didn't laugh. But he did smile. A slightly lopsided smile that lightened his eyes to silver and warmed up her insides like a Bunsen burner.

"How can I turn down...SPF 50?" he murmured.

Maybe he *was* reckless but he knew his sunscreen.

Evie waited for Faith to join her, and they started down the driveway. Faith's plodding steps conveyed her unhappiness with the situation, but Evie didn't push for conversation or attention. When Faith wanted to talk, she would.

"What did you say we're going to study?" Faith finally asked.

Evie hid a smile. *"Canis familiaris."*

Faith kicked a rock and sent it skittering down the lane. "I've never heard of that."

"It's Latin for the domestic dog," Evie said. "We're going to visit Sophie's puppies."

Faith grinned. "I think I'm going to like having you as a teacher, Miss McBride."

"This is summer school. Call me Evie."

By the time Sophie's modest, two-story house came into view several minutes later, Faith was still chattering about the puppies and how it was up to her to choose a name for her favorite.

"I've always wanted to have a dog, but Mom doesn't like it when they shed," Faith continued. "Sophie says she'll keep the one I name and I can visit it whenever I want to. That's kind of like having my own dog, isn't it?"

Evie thought it an extremely generous gesture on Sophie's part, which made her more anxious to meet the woman. And even though Faith's comment about her mother made Evie curious, she knew it wasn't the time to press Faith to talk about her family.

"There she is." Faith broke away and sprinted toward a woman kneeling in a patch of freshly turned soil. "Hi, Sophie!"

No wonder Patrick talked about her. Sophie Graham was beautiful. Blessed with classic features and smooth, porcelain skin, Sophie resembled an aging film star. Her faded housedress and scuffed gardening clogs couldn't disguise her natural grace as she rose to her feet and greeted Faith with a hug.

Faith pointed in her direction and Evie quickened her steps, hoping Sophie wouldn't mind they'd shown up without a formal invitation.

Before she could apologize, Sophie's warm smile put her at ease. "Evangeline. I'm so glad to finally meet you. Patrick talks about you and your sisters all the time."

"Dad talks about you, too," Evie said, surprised to see a hint of rose tint Sophie's cheeks.

"Can I show Evie the puppies, Sophie?"

"If we're not interrupting anything," Evie added quickly.

"Not at all. You came at just the right time. I'm ready to take a rest." Sophie swept her straw hat off and used it as a fan.

Evie's breath caught in her throat as she saw the irregular patches of silver hair on Sophie's head.

"I'm in remission, praise the Lord," Sophie said simply, and then gave Evie a mischievous wink. "Now, let's get acquainted over ice cream and puppies, shall we?"

Chapter Five

When an hour went by and Evie and Faith still hadn't returned, it occurred to Sam that his niece may have tried to sweet-talk Evie into stopping at Sophie's house.

Which meant Sophie might inadvertently reveal the real reason behind Patrick and Jacob's fishing trip.

Sam winced as the hammer missed the nail and ground the tip of his thumb against the shingle.

None of your business, he reminded himself. If Evie had a problem with her dad, she should take it up with him. Sam had his own stuff to worry about. He was one hundred percent uninvolved in the situation.

Except that Evie was Faith's tutor. And for the next few weeks, he was committed to making sure she stayed that way.

Sam sat back on his heels, trying to convince himself it wasn't necessary to look for them. Evie would be a strict teacher—the kind who wouldn't waste precious minutes of a two-hour tutoring session playing with a litter of puppies. Hopefully the reason they were late was because the search for *Canis familiaris* was taking longer than expected....

A dim memory from Biology 101 struggled to the surface. Canis. Canine. *Dog.*

Sam's shout of laughter scattered the guinea hens in the yard below.

So maybe he'd misjudged her. But he knew one thing for sure. He had to get to Sophie before Evie did.

It didn't take Evie long to understand why Faith frequently "ran away" to Sophie's house. And it wasn't just to visit the puppies or because Sophie's home, filled with simple yet comfortable furnishings, created a peaceful retreat. Sophie was the reason Faith returned. The older woman radiated a warmth and inner peace that instantly made a person feel welcome. And accepted.

"I wish I could keep all four of them," Sophie said as Faith wrestled on the braided rug with two of the more active puppies while their mother, Sadie, kept a watchful eye from her wicker basket in the corner. "A few days after my diagnosis, Sadie showed up in the yard. I knew right away she was a stray—her fur was matted, and, even pregnant, she looked like she hadn't eaten for days. I called your dad and he came over and helped me bathe her. He even offered to take her home with him, but I'd already fallen in love with her. God must have known I'd need her." Sophie smiled. "She's a very good listener."

Was Sadie the only one you fell in love with?

Evie didn't voice the question that sprang into her mind. Whenever Sophie mentioned Patrick's name, her eyes sparkled with affection. The two of them had obviously become close. But had the friendship developed into something more?

And how would she feel if it had?

The previous summer, Evie had scolded Caitlin for her strong reaction to Patrick and Sophie's friendship. If Sophie Graham brought some happiness into their dad's life, shouldn't they be supportive?

She had to admit, though, that the possibility of making room for another person in her dad's life was a little unsettling. Especially when Evie had been the one looking out for Patrick since Laura died.

"I don't know what I'd do without Jacob and Patrick," Sophie went on. "They fuss more than they ought to, but I wouldn't be able to live out here if they didn't help me keep the place up. The Lord sent those two wonderful men. I was in the hospital with complications from pneumonia, worried I'd have to sell my house, when Patrick showed up one Sunday with a group of men from his church to read to the patients. Your father got stuck with me." Sophie chuckled at the memory.

"We had a nice chat afterward and found out that we both loved antiques. The next Sunday, he introduced me to Jacob. They brought Monopoly along and convinced me to play. I don't think I ever laughed so much in my life. By the time I came home from the hospital, they'd spruced up the place and every day one of them would stop by or call to check up on me. I think they adopted me like I was a stray— just like Sadie."

Evie hid a smile. Somehow, she doubted it was an accurate comparison!

"They were a reminder that no matter what the future holds, God's already there, preparing the way. Oh, He doesn't always smooth out the rough spots in the road ahead. Those are the places we have to exercise our spiritual muscles, you know. To build our faith, so to speak. But God always provides the strength I need to keep going."

The sincerity in the words touched Evie and explained the source of the peace in Sophie's eyes. Evie knew that the woman's deep faith, the fruit of years of walking with the Lord, was another quality Patrick would have been drawn to.

A sudden movement on the stairs caught Evie's attention. The man glowering at them over the railing looked to be only a few years older than she was, but the expression on his face made him look like a cranky toddler who'd just awakened from a nap.

"Evie, this is my son, Tyson." Sophie ignored Tyson's sullen look while she made the introductions. "Tyson, this is Evie McBride, Patrick's daughter."

"Hey." His hooded stare fixed on Evie. It reminded her of a crocodile. Cold and flat.

This was Sophie's *son?*

A shudder chased up Evie's spine, but she forced a polite smile. "It's nice to meet you, Tyson."

"Evie is taking care of Beach Glass while Patrick is away on his fishing trip," Sophie told him.

"There's not much to do around here." Tyson's gaze burrowed into her. "We should hang out sometime."

A shiver coursed through her. "I'm afraid I don't have much free time. I'll either be minding the shop or tutoring Faith."

Tyson shrugged and stomped down the rest of the stairs. "I'm going out for a while."

"Ty, where—"

The door snapped Sophie's question in half.

Evie's heart went out to her. It was hard to believe someone as rude as Tyson was Sophie's flesh and blood. With his unkempt appearance and surly attitude, Tyson didn't seem to be someone Sophie could depend on. No wonder she was so grateful for Patrick and Jacob's help.

Faith broke the awkward silence as she plopped next to Sophie on the couch, the puppy draped over her arm. It raised its head and tried to lick her cheek, igniting a fit of the giggles.

Sophie smiled but Evie didn't miss the pensive look in her eyes. Compliments of Tyson. Impulsively, Evie patted Sophie's hand before rising to her feet.

"We should go back, Faith. We still need to go over your homework for tomorrow."

"I'll have to do it on the boat. Sam promised we could spend the whole day on the water. And I get to make lunch." Faith launched to her feet and put the puppy back on the rug with his littermates.

Evie kept her expression neutral. She didn't want Faith to pick up on the fact she wasn't happy with Sam for taking her out on the boat. The thought of them at the mercy of Superior's changing moods made her uneasy.

It's not your business, Evie, and Sam Cutter would be the first person to tell you so.

"Come back soon." Sophie escorted them outside. "When I talked to Patrick this morning, he asked me if I had plans to stop by Beach Glass soon and introduce myself. I can't wait to tell him that you beat me to it."

"Dad called you? *This morning?* I thought they weren't going to be able to contact us until they got to the lodge."

Sophie looked away, flustered. "We talked only a few minutes. I think he called from a gas station and the connection wasn't very good.... Look, there's Sam."

Sure enough, Sam was striding down the driveway toward them. Seeing the uncomfortable look on Sophie's face, Evie got the impression Sam's appearance provided a welcome disruption.

She tried to squelch the tiny pinprick of hurt. Why

had her dad checked in with Sophie first? It didn't make sense. Especially when Patrick knew she wanted to keep in close contact...

"Studying hard?"

The glint in Sam's eyes told Evie he was on to her.

"Don't you dare scold these sweet girls, Sam," Sophie said. "They're good company. And Sadie and the puppies love the attention."

Faith wrapped her arms around Sophie's waist and gave her a fierce hug. "We'll be back."

They said their goodbyes, and Evie and Sam fell into step together while Faith dashed ahead of them.

"*Canis familiaris,* hmm?"

Evie swallowed hard when Sam's breath stirred her hair. He was so close she could smell the pleasing blend of shower soap and afternoon sun. And a hint of coconut-scented sunscreen.

When she finally found her voice, it sounded a little breathless even to her own ears. "I thought Faith and I should take some time to get to know each other before we jumped into her lessons."

Sam slanted a look at her. "I think you know her already. It didn't take you long to figure out the way to Faith's heart is through those puppies."

Faith, several yards ahead of them, heard the word *puppies* and darted back.

"I thought of a name. I'm going to call him Rocky."

"Rocky?" Sam laughed. "Like the boxer?"

Faith nodded. "I watched the movies with Dad on cable last year. He said he liked Rocky because he never gave up."

Sam's throat closed.

Dan was giving up. The last time Sam had seen his brother, Dan had ordered the entire family to leave the room. When they'd hesitated, he'd thrown a pitcher of ice water at them. Along with a stream of angry words.

The man lying in the hospital bed had been a stranger, not the twin brother he'd wrestled, competed against and laughed with over the past thirty-two years.

Fortunately, Faith hadn't been there to witness her father's rage.

Moments before, the doctor had reminded Dan how lucky he was to be alive. But Dan had looked at him as if he'd just been given a death sentence.

Sam couldn't blame him.

Dan had been at the height of his career and the sole supporter of the family he loved. And he'd just been told he was facing months of painful rehab with no guarantee he would ever fully regain the use of his legs.

Responding to the doctor's meaningful look, they'd left Dan alone and gathered together in the family lounge. Sam had never seen Jacob look so defeated. And he'd never felt so helpless in his life. Even when Natalie, their mother, had died, he and

Dan had stuck together. Leaned on each other. Found strength in their bond as brothers.

But not this time. Nothing Sam could say or do could change the reality of the situation. And he didn't know what to do with that.

Rachel, as emotional as Dan was easygoing, had clung to him. It would have been better if she'd been able to cry. At least tears could be dried. Sam had had no idea how to comfort a heart totally emptied by grief.

He had lain in bed that night, despair lapping at the edges of his soul. He'd tried to pray, but it had felt hypocritical. He wasn't sure if God would even recognize his voice. It wasn't as if they talked on a regular basis.

A week went by and Dan had still refused to see them. Faith had started to blame "the adults" for not allowing her to visit her father. Her close relationship with her mother had deteriorated, and she'd alternated between outright defiance and long, stubborn silences.

The hospital had transferred Dan to a private care facility to start rehab, and the doctor warned them that Dan's attitude would be a pivotal part of his recovery. The hospital social worker had told them Dan was battling depression and had compassionately suggested they give him a few weeks to adjust to his new surroundings before visiting again.

Jacob had reluctantly returned to Cooper's Landing. Sam used up more vacation time and had stayed longer, watching in disbelief as Dan became verbally abusive to the nurses and refused to cooperate with his physical therapists. His bitter tirades had kept Rachel on the verge of tears.

Sam had always been able to encourage his brother. Even to bully him, if the situation called for it. But for the first time in his life, Sam had sensed his presence was causing more harm than good. The bitterness in Dan's eyes every time Sam visited had weighed him down with guilt. He was able to walk while Dan was confined to a wheelchair, and Sam couldn't find a way to break down that barrier between them.

When Rachel had overheard him talking to Jacob on the phone about taking the boat out for a few weeks, she'd begged him to take Faith along. Torn between meeting the needs of both her daughter and her husband, she'd said she needed time to concentrate on Dan and encourage his recovery.

Sam had balked. He'd wanted to be alone. His world had shrunk to the size of the hospital and he was tired of sterile white walls, the hum of machines and plastic tubing that kept a man alive but couldn't make him want to *live*. He struggled between feeling selfish for leaving Rachel alone with Dan and the overwhelming need to escape.

In the end, he'd agreed to take Faith with him.

He'd tried to talk to her about her dad but she'd refused. Somewhere along the way, Sam had become a member of the opposing team. An hour didn't go by when he didn't second-guess his decision to bring her along.

"I think Rocky is a great name. Don't you, Sam?"

With a start, Evie's voice and the touch of her hand on his arm pulled Sam out of the shadowy path his memories had lured him down. Faith hadn't voluntarily talked about Dan since they'd arrived in Cooper's Landing. She'd even rebuffed her grandfather whenever he'd tried to talk about her dad. Now, because of Evie's gentle prompt, he realized Faith was watching him, waiting patiently for his response. She wasn't just asking if he liked the name. There was another question in her eyes.

Is Dad going to be like Rocky? Or is he going to give up?

He couldn't answer her. It wasn't fair to give her false hope, yet he didn't want to be the one to crush it, either.

"I think you should take a picture of you and Rocky and send it to your dad." Evie bravely stepped into the silence.

"Really?" Faith glanced at him for affirmation. "The nurse told me the last time I called there was a bulletin board by his bed. She said Dad has my letter on it."

Sam had had no idea Faith had written to her father or called the rehab center. Guilt washed over him. He'd failed his brother and now he was failing his niece. He struggled to find his voice. "Evie's right. I think he'd like that."

"Does that mean we can study *Canis familiaris* again tomorrow?" Faith's tentative smile was like seeing a beam of sunlight peek through the clouds.

"You'll have to discuss that with your teacher."

Faith sprinted ahead of them and Sam held his breath, expecting Evie to hit him with a hundred questions now. And she'd be within her rights. He should have been honest with her the night he'd asked her to be Faith's tutor. He'd convinced himself Evie didn't need to know their family business but the truth was, he'd always kept a tight rein on his emotions and Dan's accident had stirred them up. Brought them to the surface. Even saying his brother's name had the potential to let those feelings loose, and he couldn't risk breaking down in front of a complete stranger.

Evie didn't say a word but one look at the set of her shoulders told him everything. He should have told her there was more to Faith's discontent than homework.

"Dan was…is…a police officer, and he was injured in an…accident." It wasn't the whole truth, but Sam didn't know how else to describe what had happened. His jaw tightened. *Someone deliberately tried to kill my brother?* Too harsh. And it would only raise more questions.

"I'm sorry."

The simple words threw him off balance. He'd expected questions. Maybe even accusations. What he wasn't prepared for was the compassion he heard in Evie's voice. And it nearly undid him.

Sam retreated behind the walls he'd put up to stave off the pain of the past few months. He felt a rush of relief when the cabin came into view.

When Evie reached her car, she opened the passenger-side door and hoisted her gigantic bag inside. He caught a glimpse of a package of gum and a box of bandages.

Bitterness welled up, catching him by surprise.

So Evie McBride thought the contents of her duffel-size purse meant she was prepared for anything. It was too bad there wasn't something in it that could fix messed-up lives.

Chapter Six

I've been praying for Sam. And Faith.

The words scrolled through Evie's mind every time she woke up during the night.

In March, her father had asked her to pray for a friend and his family. He'd only shared a few details. The friend's son was a Chicago police officer who'd been shot while responding to a call. After surgery to remove a bullet near his spine, the doctors were still uncertain whether he'd ever walk again. He had a wife and twelve-year-old daughter. And a devastated twin brother.

"No one in the family is a believer, Evie," Patrick had told her. "They don't know how to comfort each other or how to *be* comforted. Instead of coming together, the family is splintering apart."

Evie had added them to her prayers even though she'd struggled with the circumstances. Another parent had chosen a dangerous profession and now a family had to suffer the consequences of that decision.

She'd had no idea the man she'd been lifting up in prayer for the past three months had been Jacob Cutter. And the child she'd asked God to comfort wasn't a nameless, faceless little girl. It was Faith. And the twin brother, Sam.

As daylight filtered through the sheer curtains, Evie gave up on sleep. She sat up in bed and wrapped her arms around her knees.

Lord, now I know why you brought me here. And why Sam asked me to tutor Faith. Give me wisdom to know how to encourage her. I wasn't much older than Faith when Mom died. I know what it's like to have your whole world turned upside down and not understand why.

Reveal yourself to them. Show them that even though the situation might seem hopeless, they can find hope in you.

Patrick had told her that none of the Cutter family were believers, but Evie had confidence God was at work. His timing was always perfect and there had to be a reason why Patrick's fishing trip and her arrival in Cooper's Landing had corresponded with Faith and Sam's trip.

Evie remembered Sam's expression when Faith had mentioned her dad. For a split second, the bleakness in Sam's eyes had reflected all the pain and anger and helplessness he felt.

Strengthen Sam, too, Lord.

* * *

Evie was closing up the shop for the day when a van pulled in and a stocky young man jumped out of the driver's seat, intercepting her on her way to the cottage.

Evie hadn't had many customers over the course of the day. If only his timing would have been better! When Patrick called, she wanted to be able to tell him she was single-handedly reducing the store's inventory. "I'm sorry. We're closed."

"Are you Evie McBride? Patrick's daughter?"

Evie paused. "Yes."

"I'm Seth. Seth Lansky? The computer tech? Mr. McBride hired me to install a new software program."

Computer tech? Evie's gaze traveled over the man's husky frame. In a flannel-lined plaid shirt and heavy boots, he looked more like pictures she'd seen of the legendary Paul Bunyan than someone who spent his days at a keyboard.

"Dad didn't mention you were coming over." Not that it was unusual for her dad to forget something. The day before he'd left, she'd caught him wandering around the house looking for his glasses. They'd been tucked in the front pocket of his shirt the whole time.

"I couldn't tell him the exact day I'd be stopping by," Seth explained. "Emergency calls get priority."

That sounded legitimate. Evie glanced over his shoulder at the vehicle parked in the driveway. It didn't have a logo painted on it but that didn't mean anything. Sleepy little Cooper's Landing wasn't exactly on the cutting edge when it came to business practices. The local post office and Ruby's Beauty Salon operated out of the same building.

"I was just about to leave for a few hours."

Seth scratched a ragged thumbnail against the stubble on his chin. "If I don't take a look at it now, I'm not sure when I can come back around. Mr. McBride seemed pretty anxious to get it taken care of. Shouldn't take very long."

Evie glanced at her watch. Four-fifteen. She was already late for her meeting with Faith.

"I suppose it's all right."

"Great." Seth flashed an engaging smile and followed her inside. Evie led the way past the kitchen to the room her dad had converted into an office when he'd moved in.

"Here you—" Evie turned the doorknob and frowned. It was locked. "That's strange. Dad never locks anything."

"There must be a key around somewhere."

"I'll look in the kitchen."

When Evie returned a few minutes later with the ring of keys she'd found hanging on a hook by sink, Seth had his back to her, talking on a cell phone.

"I'm surprised you get reception. Half the time, mine won't work."

Seth gave a visible start and snapped the phone shut. "This one didn't, either."

Evie sifted through the keys, looking for one that

might fit. "You'll have your work cut out for you. Dad hates computers. The PC my sisters and I bought him a few years ago when he opened the shop is already outdated. I tried to teach him how to use it but I'm pretty sure he kept his old typewriter as a backup. Here. I think this is the right one...." Evie choked as the door to Patrick's office drifted open.

"Looks like your dad got the hang of it," Seth drawled.

"I can't believe this," Evie murmured, studying the expensive flat-screen monitor she *knew* hadn't been part of the package they'd bought for Patrick. There was also a combination printer and—Evie blinked— *fax machine?*

Seth didn't answer as he sat down at the desk and pressed the power button.

Evie lingered, still uncertain whether she should leave him alone in the house. But Faith needed her. "I'll be back in a little while."

Seth chuckled. "Don't worry about me. Like I said, this shouldn't take long."

Evie slung her bag over her shoulder and made a quick detour to the garage before leaving for her afternoon tutoring session.

When she pulled into the Cutters' driveway, she was encouraged to see Faith sitting on the step, waiting for her to arrive. And relieved they'd made it safely back to shore.

Thank you, Lord.

Instead of saying hello, Faith greeted her with a gloomy announcement. "Sam says I have to work on my math assignments first."

"Really?" Evie opened the trunk of the car. "I hate to veto your uncle, but the teacher sets the schedule. We're having gym class first."

Faith peeked into the trunk and her eyes lit up when she saw the basketball hoop. "Is that for me?"

"It's for us. I warned you I was a science geek, right? You'll have to take it easy on me until I learn the rules."

"We can mount it above the garage door. I'll get Sam." Faith bounded away before Evie could stop her.

Evie's heart gave a strange little flutter when Sam emerged from the cabin. They must have recently come off the lake because his hair curled damply at the base of his neck. His casual clothing should have looked scruffy, but Sam wore the threadbare chambray shirt and faded jeans with casual ease. He could have graced the cover of any popular boating magazine.

Once again, Evie wondered what he did for a living. He'd walked across the roof with catlike grace the day before, but his skin didn't have the weathered look of someone who worked outside all day. Although his biceps could have been honed by construction work...

"Heads up, Evie!" Faith's cheerful warning rang across the yard.

The basketball sailed toward her, and Evie instinctively lifted her hands. And missed. The force of the ball against her abdomen winded her.

"Wow." She gasped the word. "There's a lot of power in that pass."

Faith grinned. "I'll get the ladder."

Sam stared after his niece in disbelief. "Who is she and what did she do with my niece? That is *not* the girl who was on the boat with me. The girl with me today refused to talk and deliberately left out the jelly on my peanut-butter and *jelly* sandwich."

Evie's soft laugh rippled through him. "You don't know how many times I've heard variations of that question at parent-teacher conferences."

The sound of her laughter never failed to surprise Sam. It was…young. Jacob had mentioned Patrick's youngest daughter was only twenty-six, but the serious blue eyes and conservative clothing made her seem older. Most women wore hats as a fashion statement, but Sam had a hunch that Evie had chosen the wide-brimmed straw hat to protect her from the sun. Probably because she'd given *him* her sunblock. Today she'd kept the cardigan but traded in her skirt for a pair of pleated khakis. And the flat-soled leather shoes on her feet weren't exactly the kind of footwear endorsed by the NBA.

Sam nudged Evie aside as she reached into the trunk of the car and wrestled with a rusty basketball hoop. "Gym class. You do have some interesting teaching methods, Miss McBride."

"Thank you."

Sam wasn't sure it was a compliment. They had two weeks to bring Faith's grades back up. So far the only books he'd seen were the ones he'd fished out of Faith's laundry basket that morning.

"I can play basketball with her anytime—"

Evie tossed the ball to him. "Great. Let's get this net up."

Not exactly what he'd meant. "Ah, maybe I didn't mention how much homework Faith has. She took it pretty hard when her dad got hurt. She stopped caring. About school. About…everything. You've got your work cut out for you over the next two weeks. To be quite honest, I don't know if there's time for puppies and basketball."

"Those are the things Faith cares about. We're going to *make* time for them. Everything else will fall into place. You'll see."

"You're the teacher."

Evie's chin lifted. "I'm glad we got that settled."

Sam expected Evie to sit on the sidelines. Maybe look over Faith's assignments while she had the opportunity. But no. She'd joined in the game with an enthusiasm that amazed him. The woman had two left hands and feet, but what she lacked in athletic ability she made up for in effort.

"You're going to have blisters on your blisters,"

Sam murmured as they crouched face-to-face in the center of the driveway in a battle for control of the ball.

Evie blew a wisp of hair out of her eyes. "Between the shin splints and the torn ligaments I won't even notice them."

Sam couldn't prevent the rusty bark of laughter that rolled out. And it surprised him. Maybe Faith wasn't the only one who had forgotten how to laugh over the past few months.

He had to admit Evie was a genius when it came to kids. Somehow she'd known exactly what his niece needed. Faith lived and breathed sports, but she'd quit the track team after Dan was injured. Not only had she walked away from something she loved, but she'd lost the physical outlet to deal with the additional stress on their family.

And he'd been totally oblivious to all that. Until now. For Faith's sake, he decided to trust Evie's unorthodox teaching methods.

"Ready, Evie?" Faith's eyes gleamed with the light of competition as she gave the basketball an impressive spin on the tip of her index finger.

"Ready, *Evie?*" Sam repeated in disbelief. "Haven't you ever heard the saying blood is thicker than water?"

"It depends on who's grading your papers," Evie retorted.

Feeling more lighthearted than he had in weeks, Sam knocked the ball out of Faith's hand and went in for a layup. Evie came out of nowhere and stole the ball, lobbing it toward the net. It hit the backboard and swished through the hoop.

Faith whooped in delight at the stunned look on Evie's face.

"Beginner's luck," Sam muttered as he jumped up and caught the rebound.

Family loyalty aside, Faith gave Evie encouragement and advice as they played. Somehow Evie had reversed their roles. She looked to Faith to teach her the rules of the game. Trusted her commands. Accepted correction.

Her strategy, Sam acknowledged, was brilliant. Evie didn't expect to win Faith's trust and respect, she wanted to earn it.

Faith would have played until dark if Sam hadn't noticed Evie's slight limp and called the game. And he didn't miss the grateful look Evie shot in his direction.

"Sam, I'm going to shower and work on my math for a while, okay?" Faith took one more shot from the makeshift free-throw line and did a little victory dance when it swept through the net. "You played a great game, Evie. Don't let anyone tell you you're just a science geek." She gave her a cheeky smile and dashed into the house.

"Did my niece just say she was going to work on her math? Without empty threats or shameless bribes?"

"She did." Evie took a folded tissue out of the pocket of her khakis and blotted her forehead. "She's a great kid, Sam. You'll get through this."

Sam had a feeling she wasn't referring only to adolescence and her next words confirmed it.

"I know about your brother. Dad asked me to pray for your family when it happened, but I didn't realize it was *you*. Not until yesterday."

"You've been *praying* for us?"

"Since March," Evie confirmed.

Three months ago, and Dan was still on a downward spiral. His lips twisted. "I wish I could tell you it's helped. Dan isn't walking yet."

"God is more interested in healing hearts than bodies," Evie said.

The simple words blindsided him.

"I'll be back tomorrow afternoon." Evie walked toward the car but Sam beat her to it and opened the driver's-side door.

"I'm going to toss some steaks on the grill. Why don't you stay for supper?" Sam had no idea which wire in his brain had short-circuited and disengaged his mouth from his brain.

Evie shook her head. "I can't."

No apologies. No excuses. Maybe he'd been impulsive to ask her to stay, but Sam still felt a stab of disappointment at her blunt refusal. He told himself it wasn't unusual to want to know a little more about the woman he'd hired to be Faith's tutor—but part of him chided himself for not being completely honest.

The truth was, Evie McBride intrigued him.

* * *

Sam reached the phone on the third ring. It was within Faith's reach but she was stretched out on the sofa with her eyes closed, headphones firmly in place.

After Evie had left, she'd retreated back into her shell. Lake Superior, for all its changing moods, had nothing on adolescent girls.

"Hello?"

A harsh crackle grated in his ear.

"Sam? This is…Patrick… Evie…needs help… Think we've…got a problem on your end." Static distorted the words and Sam frowned. "Take care…her."

"Patrick, I can barely hear you," Sam said. "What did you say about Evie?"

Patrick's voice broke up again and Sam felt a surge of frustration. "One more time, Patrick. The connection is terrible. Are you and Dad at the lodge yet?"

"Go…Evie. Might…danger." The line went dead.

"Patrick?" Sam hit Redial and got a busy signal.

Now what?

Sam tried to convince himself he'd imagined the word *danger*. But why had Patrick called him instead of Jacob?

Sam glanced at his watch. Seven o'clock. Evie had left half an hour ago. She'd think he was crazy if showed up out of the blue to check on her. And he'd have a lot of explaining to do if he told her Patrick had called *him*. He still hadn't found the right time to tell her what their fathers were up to. The truth was, he'd been hoping he wouldn't have to.

Ten minutes crawled by as Sam paced the living room, waiting for Patrick to call back. Finally, he shook Faith's knee to get her attention.

"I'm going to drop you off at Sophie's for a few minutes, okay? I've got an errand to run."

Faith, eager to play with Rocky, didn't question him.

When he got to Evie's ten minutes later, he saw a van parked close to the house. His stomach knotted. Beach Glass was closed for the day, and he doubted Evie had made friends in the short time she'd been staying at the house.

He knocked on the door but didn't wait for someone to answer it. Giving in to an overwhelming sense of urgency, he turned the handle and went inside.

Chapter Seven

"Miss McBride?" Seth poked his head into the kitchen. "Wow. Something smells good."

"Garlic bread." Evie wiped her hands on the old-fashioned pinafore apron she'd found in a box of linens at the shop. When she'd gotten back from Sam's, she'd found Seth still hard at work in Patrick's office.

Feeling a little awkward with someone else in the house, she'd reheated some leftover pasta from the night before and lingered in the kitchen, hoping Seth would finish soon. She wanted the house to herself to sort through the strange jumble of emotions she felt whenever Sam Cutter cruised the perimeter of her personal space.

She drew a deep breath. Even when he wasn't around, the man had the most unsettling way of creeping into her thoughts. "Are you finished?"

"No. As a matter of fact, I've got a little problem.

Your dad gave me his password but he must have changed it and forgotten to tell me. Think you can take a look? Most people use familiar words. Birthdays. Names of children. That sort of thing."

"I can try." Evie followed him into the office and sat down in the chair.

"Here's what I've got so far." He pushed a piece of paper in front of her. "Charlotte. Sara. Jo. Do you see a pattern there? Are they middle names? Old girlfriends?"

Evie didn't think the last comment particularly funny.

"There's more than one password?"

Seth smiled and shrugged. "You know Patrick."

That she did. Her dad probably thought he needed a password to protect his password.

"They aren't middle names." *Or old girlfriends.* She studied the names a few more seconds and started to laugh. "I can't believe Dad remembered. We had an aquarium when I was growing up. Every time we got a new fish, my sisters and I named it after the heroine of a book we were reading at the time. Charlotte is from *Charlotte's Web*. Sara is in *A Little Princess* and Jo is one of the March sisters in *Little Women*."

Seth leaned closer, his eyes strangely intent. "What's the next one?"

"Let me think…." Evie bit her lip. Nancy Drew? No, Caitlin had vetoed that one. It had been a blue Betta fish and according to Caitlin's logic, a fish named Nancy Drew had to be *red*. No wonder she'd started an image consulting business after graduating from college.

"Evie?"

The sound of Sam's voice startled her. She twisted in the chair and saw him standing in the doorway behind her.

"I knocked but you must not have heard me."

"Sam. What are you doing here?" Once again her first thought was for her father. She rose to her feet but Seth's hand snaked out and caught her wrist.

"I've got two more calls to make this evening, Miss McBride." The faint bite in the words surprised her. Seth hadn't mentioned other appointments. And he certainly hadn't seemed to be in a hurry to finish up before now.

Evie gently tugged her wrist free. "This will only take a minute."

"Sure." Seth's lips worked into a smile. "No problem."

Sam leaned against the door frame and stuck his hands in his pockets. "I forgot to give you Faith's reading list for her book reports when you were over this afternoon. I saw the lights on and decided to drop it off."

Not exactly an emergency, Evie thought. Maybe he'd had another argument with Faith and wanted to talk about it. "I'll be right back, Seth."

As soon as they were in the hall, Sam took hold of

her arm and guided her toward the door. When Evie opened her mouth to protest, Sam tapped his finger against her lips, shocking her into silence.

Once they were outside, she pulled away from him and planted her hands on her hips. "What do you think you're doing?"

"Who is that guy?" Sam asked tersely.

"Seth Lansky. Dad hired him to install some software."

"Your dad set up the appointment? He told you about it before he left?"

"No. He forgot. But that's nothing new—"

"Evie. Think about it." Sam's eyes held hers intently. "Patrick wouldn't hire someone to install software. Not when he's got a computer-savvy daughter coming to stay at his house for two weeks."

Evie's mouth went dry. "What are you getting at?"

"What did Seth ask you to do?"

Evie noticed Sam Cutter had an annoying habit of answering a question with a question. "Dad isn't very knowledgeable about computers. He set up multiple passwords when one would have been sufficient." There. That should prove her point.

"Maybe he set up multiple passwords on purpose." Sam edged her into the shadows between the house and the shop. Evie squeaked as he backed her against the wall, angling his body so she was hidden from view and bracing a hand on either side of her.

"That's crazy. The only thing Dad keeps on his

computer is his personal budget and the financial records for Beach Glass."

"If this guy is *installing* software, why does he need to access your dad's files?"

Evie stared up at him. "I don't know."

Disbelief and fear skimmed across Evie's face.

Good, Sam thought. Now they were even. The vehicle parked in the driveway had made him uneasy, but finding Evie sitting at the desk, with an all-star wrestler wannabe leaning over her, had shaved ten years off his life.

"When did this guy show up? Did you ask him for any identification?"

"Right before I left this afternoon," Evie whispered.

Her failure to answer his second question was an answer in and of itself. He'd lecture her about that later. Right now he had to determine if Patrick's phone call and Lansky's showing up was a big fat coincidence.

"I'm going to take a look inside his van." He took a step forward and so did Evie.

"I'm not staying here."

"Now isn't the time to be nervous. You missed that opportunity. It would have been when a stranger came up to the door and you let him in your house." He knew he'd already made his point, but he couldn't help it. His heart was still doing jumping jacks in his chest, and he blamed it on the naive redhead standing in front of him. Apparently, there were times when her warm heart overrode her cautious nature.

He took another step forward. So did Evie.

"You can't spy on him alone. What if he sees you and you get hurt?"

Thanks for the vote of confidence, Sam thought wryly. "I'll be fine. Stay here and make yourself invisible. I'll be right back."

This time when he took a step forward, she stayed put.

Sam sidled around the house, pausing to take a quick look in the window. Seth had taken Evie's place at the desk and it looked like he was trying to figure out the password himself. Sam watched long enough to see him engage in the good old "hunt and peck" method of keyboarding. If this guy turned out to be a computer tech, Sam moonlighted as a gourmet chef. And everyone who knew him knew he lived on takeout.

He worked his way over to the van and tried the door. Locked. That was interesting. Apparently Seth wasn't as trusting as the woman who'd let him into her house. Keeping a wary eye on the front door, he circled the van.

And bumped into someone coming around the other side.

"I thought I told you to stay put." Sam said goodbye to another ten years. Only catching a whiff of a familiar floral scent in the air had prevented him from tackling the person first and asking questions later.

"Will this help?" The faint glow of a penlight illuminated Evie's face.

"As a matter of fact, it will." Sam plucked the key ring out of her hand, not prepared for the weight of it. "What do you have on here? A hammer? Never mind. Let me guess. *The essentials.*"

He traced the interior of the van with the tiny beam of light. Crumpled potato-chip bags, soda cups and empty paper sacks littered the seat and floor.

"Where fast-food lunches go to die," Sam murmured. "Well, we know he's got high cholesterol. Let's take a look in the back and see what else we can find out about Mr. Lansky." He pressed the light against the back window and his blood chilled.

Okay, Dad, what have you and Patrick gotten your-selves into?

And more important, what had they gotten Evie into?

Evie stood on her tiptoes, her nose pressed against the glass as she peered inside. "What is all that?"

"Diving equipment."

Sam took a quick inventory and what he saw didn't make him feel any better. The gear wasn't amateur, weekend-warrior stuff. The front seat of the van might have resembled a college frat house, but the equipment in the back was practically arranged in alphabetical order. Expensive cameras. Oxygen tanks. Wet suits. And a very lethal-looking spear gun.

He lowered the light before Evie spotted it.

Sam's mind raced over possible scenarios and

none of them included a computer tech. What he did have were two AWOL senior citizens with delusions of grandeur trying to track down clues to a sunken treasure. A frantic phone call from Patrick. A guy trying to access Patrick's computer files…and Evie somewhere in the middle.

The front door opened, tripping the motion light in the yard. Sam dropped to his knees, taking Evie with him.

She struggled against him and Sam saw the outrage and mistrust in her wide blue eyes. She didn't trust *him?* She let some guy into her house without asking for ID, and now *he* was the bad guy?

"Let me go." She struggled against him.

"Sorry." Sam eased away from her. "It looks like Mr. Lansky is done for the night and until we know if he's legit, I don't want him to catch us checking out his van. Time to work on your acting skills."

Sam did it again. He grabbed her hand, kept low to the ground and pulled her into the woods bordering the driveway.

"Play along," he whispered.

"Play along with what—" The words died as Sam rose to his feet, wrapped his arm around her waist and nuzzled her hair. Evie's feet melted to the ground, but somehow Sam managed to nudge her out of the shadows.

"He's watching." Sam breathed the words in her ear. "Let him think we were taking a romantic stroll."

Evie swallowed hard as she and Sam stepped into the light. Seth stood beside the van, scowling at them. When she'd met him that afternoon, Seth had reminded her of a teddy bear, but now his barrel-shaped frame and thick arms looked more menacing than cuddly.

Sam stiffened, as if he were bracing for a confrontation. Both men topped six feet, but even though Sam was muscular, he lacked Seth's solid bulk.

Evie had never been a flirt—she didn't even have a clue *how* to flirt—but she smiled playfully up at Sam and linked her arm through his. "Saturday sounds great.… Oh, hi, Seth. I'm sorry it took us so long but we had some things to…discuss."

She didn't have to pretend to be embarrassed that he'd caught them. She could *feel* her freckles getting hot.

For one heart-stopping moment, Seth stared at them, his fists clenched at his sides as he took a step closer.

"You two go ahead and finish on the computer, Evie." Sam tucked a strand of hair behind her ear and gave her a smile. "I'll make some popcorn and put in a movie."

Evie had never had a man look at her like that before—even if he *was* pretending. Her older sisters both had had their share of romances, but Evie had shied away from dating. In high school and college, she'd preferred reading to socializing and knew her serious nature turned off guys who wanted to have fun. Self-conscious of her pale skin, flaming red hair and gangly figure, Evie had discovered that even though she couldn't make herself physically disappear, she could get lost in the pages of a book. She could join adventurous people who didn't wear cardigans or carry dental floss in their purse.

"Honey?"

Honey?

Sam squeezed her hand and his eyes flashed a warning, reminding her to play her part.

Evie recovered and gave him an adoring look. "All right…dear."

Sam made a choking sound and Evie turned to Seth, giving him a bright smile. "Should we all go back inside? I'm sure I'll remember the password but I can always call my sisters. Maybe they'll know."

Seth looked as if he'd just swallowed broken glass. "I don't want to take up any more of your time. I'll finish the job when your dad gets back from his fishing trip."

He unlocked the van and climbed inside. As the van rattled down the driveway, Evie realized she was still clinging to Sam's arm. She let go and stepped away from him, crossing her arms over her chest.

"I think he bought it." Sam exhaled. "Or maybe he decided your house wasn't big enough for the both of us."

"What. Is. Going. On?"

Sam raked a hand through his hair. "I wish I knew," he muttered.

The man who'd given her the adoring, lopsided smile had disappeared. The man who replaced him looked as though he'd rather be treading water in Lake Superior than be with her. And it stung.

"You show up here out of the blue. Some guy is trying to access Dad's computer files. Why?" Evie's voice cracked on the last word. *Terrific.* She sounded like a hysterical female.

Sam pivoted and strode toward the house, leaving Evie no choice but to chase after him while he gave her a brief explanation. "I didn't show up out of the blue. Your dad called me."

"Dad? Why would he call *you?*"

"Believe me—I have as many questions as you do. The connection was bad but Patrick said you might be in danger. That's why I stopped by. And it's a good thing I did." He gave her a dark look.

"That's silly. You must have misunderstood him. Why would I be in danger?" A thought whisked through her, sending her heart speeding into overdrive. "Do you think Seth is planning to rob the antique shop? But why would he need Dad's password? Is *Dad* in trouble?" Fear spiraled through her. "I'm going to call the lodge and talk to him myself…."

Sam stopped so abruptly, Evie slammed into him. It was like running into a telephone pole.

"It might help if your dad was *at* the lodge."

"That must be where he called you from. According to my itinerary, they should have arrived there at six o'clock."

"Your *itinerary?*" he repeated.

"I plotted out their trip. Based on mileage. Number of stops. Packing the canoes and paddling to the island. My calculations could be off, but not by more than fifteen minutes."

Sam stared at her as if she'd spoken in a different language.

"That's it. We're going to Sophie's."

"What? Why?" She scrambled away from him when he reached for her hand. She was tired of being towed around like a piece of wheeled luggage.

"Because our fathers are having a delayed midlife crisis, that's why."

Evie managed to grab her purse as Sam took hold of her elbow and hustled her out the door.

Chapter Eight

"Oh, dear." Sophie took one look at Sam's face and put her hand to her throat. "Come in."

"Where's Faith?"

"She fell asleep on the couch. I think the puppies wore her out."

"We need to talk to you." Sam lowered his voice. "Is Tyson here?"

Sophie shook her head, casting an anxious glance at Evie. He didn't blame her for being concerned. If possible, Evie's skin looked more pale than usual. He'd expected to be bombarded with questions on the car ride over to Sophie's, but Evie had sat quietly, her hands twisting the straps of the gigantic purse in her lap.

"Come into the sitting room." Sophie bustled ahead of them. "We can talk there without disturbing Faith. Would you like something to drink? Tea? Coffee?"

"Sophie, I don't think—" Sophie speared him with

a meaningful glance at Evie, who'd wilted into the worn velvet settee in the corner.

"Coffee." He had a feeling they were in for a long night.

He reined in his impatience until Sophie returned with a tray crowded with delicate china cups and a plate of paper-thin lemon cookies.

Sophie dropped two sugar cubes into Evie's cup before settling into a chair opposite them.

Sam had never been good at small talk, and he wasn't in the mood for it now. His stomach still clenched at the thought of finding Evie alone with the guy who'd managed to charm his way into Patrick's private office. Except Lansky hadn't gotten what he'd been looking for. Which meant he might come back.

"I got a call from Patrick tonight, Sophie. Before we got cut off, he said Evie might be in danger. When I went to the house to check on her, there was a man with her. A Seth Lansky. He told Evie that Patrick had hired him to work on his computer but it was clear he was really trying to get into the files." Sam watched the color ebb out of Sophie's face and felt a stab of guilt. Jacob would string him up for confronting her like this, but Sophie was the only person who might be able to explain Patrick's urgent phone call.

"You told me that Dad and Patrick were meeting with a friend about finding a ship that sank in Superior. Is there something you *didn't* tell me?"

Sophie's hands fluttered in her lap. "I'm afraid there's a lot I didn't tell you."

"We're listening." Sam softened his tone, reminding himself that Sophie had gone through a lot over the past year. But he had to make sure Evie was safe before he'd let her go back to the house alone.

"What are you two talking about?" Evie broke in. "Dad and Jacob are on a *fishing* trip. He never said a thing about meeting a friend…or searching for a…*ship*."

"He didn't want to worry you." Sophie sighed. "And the only reason I mentioned it to Sam the other day was because I thought Jacob had told him."

Evie leaned forward. "Told him what? Where *are* they?"

Sophie paused and closed her eyes. When she opened them, it was obvious she'd come to a decision.

"Shortly before I found out I had cancer, I'd started researching my family genealogy. I knew there'd been a scandal a long time ago. My grandmother always referred to it as the Graham family curse. It made me curious and I started contacting distant relatives, trying to find out what they remembered about it. Finally, I discovered a distant cousin who was thrilled to get rid of a box of old papers she'd had in her attic for years.

"My great-grandmother's journal was in it, along with letters she and her daughter-in-law, Dorothea, had exchanged. Dorothea and her husband had had a rocky marriage, and she blamed my great-grand-father, Matthew Graham. Apparently Matthew had been branded a thief and betrayed people who trusted him. Dorothea believed Matthew's actions had marked the family and no one would ever be free of them. I think that was why my grandmother referred to the scandal as a curse. But for me, it became a blessing. In the middle of reading through the journal and Dorothea's letters, I found out I had cancer. But I didn't feel hopeless because God had given me a purpose." Sophie paused and took a deep breath. "I decided to find out the truth. What really happened and if Matthew Graham was guilty or not."

"But what does this have to do with Dad? And Jacob?" Evie asked in confusion.

"They offered to help me."

Evie closed her eyes, relieved. "Dad is helping you research your family history? That makes sense. He'll spend hours sifting through books—"

"He's not looking through books," Sam interrupted. "He and my dad are looking for a ship. Or, to be more exact, something *on* the ship."

"That's impossible. Dad doesn't know the first thing about that kind of stuff." Evie looked to Sophie for reassurance, but the expression on the older woman's face caused a fresh crop of goose bumps to rise on her arms. Was she really supposed to believe that her quiet, scholarly father had gotten mixed up in a crazy hunt for a sunken treasure? If he had, she didn't blame Sophie. It had to be Jacob Cutter's fault.

"Sam is right," Sophie admitted. "They're looking for the *Noble.*"

"What do you know about it?" Sam asked.

"Not a lot. According to Dorothea's letters, a ship came over from England in 1890. Over the past few months, Patrick and I searched through dozens of old newspaper clippings. We found several references to the *Noble,* a wooden steamer that sank in October the same year. It went down in heavy fog and only one person survived."

"Your great-grandfather."

Sophie nodded. "Matthew worked in a logging camp and his boss had hired him to go to England and escort Lady Dale Carrington back to the United States. Lady Dale's father had arranged for her to marry Randall Lawrence, the son of a lumber baron. She brought a wedding gift from her family with her. A dowry, if you will. I can't find a specific reference as to what it was. Maybe jewelry. A family heirloom of some kind. Whatever it was, it must have been extremely valuable. The loss of it stirred up more of a fuss in the Lawrence family than the loss of a prospective bride.

"Matthew claimed Lady Dale's dowry sank with the ship, but they found her betrothal ring in his possession. It was all the proof Randall needed. He accused Matthew of saving himself and the treasure.

Matthew denied it, but his reputation was ruined. A few years later, he married my great-grandmother but something had happened to him. He drank heavily and couldn't keep a job. They barely scratched out a living."

"Not exactly the kind of life a man harboring a treasure would choose," Sam said. "If he'd managed to survive and keep the dowry, he would have moved far away and put it to good use."

Sophie gave him an approving smile. "My thought exactly."

"Who knows about the *Noble?*" Sam asked suddenly. "Is it common knowledge there was something valuable on board?"

"I don't think so. No one in my family ever said a word about a treasure—I didn't even know what Matthew had been accused of stealing until I read Dorothea's letters. She was the first one who had mentioned a dowry. The newspaper articles only reported that the entire crew had gone missing, their bodies never recovered. Some of my distant relatives know I've been researching the Graham family history, but only Patrick and Jacob know specific details about the *Noble* and Lady Dale's dowry."

Listening to their exchange, Evie remembered the diving gear in the back of Seth's van and a knot formed in her throat. "Are there people who look for sunken ships that might have a treasure on board?"

Sophie hesitated. "There are laws that protect

wrecks from being salvaged in areas designated as underwater preserves."

"But what if the *Noble* sank outside a preserve?"

"Permits would need to be filed." Sam answered the question. "But some people might bypass that little detail."

"But Sophie said no one knows for sure where the *Noble* went down," Evie reminded him.

"Jacob's old friend, Bruce Mullins, is a diver. He's been credited with discovering several important wrecks in the Great Lakes over the past decade," Sophie said. "He's familiar with Superior and would know if there's a possibility the *Noble* can be found. I know Patrick and Jacob made it clear to Bruce that everything they told him was to be held in the strictest confidence."

Sam scrubbed the palms of his hands against his face. "I'm pretty sure someone knows about it now," he said grimly. "Do you have any idea why they'd be interested in Patrick's computer files, Sophie?"

Sophie bit her lip. "The day before they left, Patrick said he had a surprise for me. Something to celebrate my six-month checkup. He wouldn't tell me what it was, but maybe he figured out where the *Noble* sank."

"He's been documenting your research on his computer?"

"Dad hates computers." Evie felt the need to point it out. Again. Patrick may have helped Sophie pore over old newspaper clippings, but if she knew her dad, he'd taken notes using his trusty ballpoint pen and paper.

Sophie slid an apologetic look in her direction. "That's not quite true—he's actually quite knowledgeable about them. He also scanned Dorothea's letters and pages from the journal into his files. I have everything locked up, but Patrick thought we should have copies. I let him handle that part of it. Tyson has a computer but I never bothered with one."

Evie didn't think her dad bothered with them, either.

Sudden tears stung Evie's eyes and made her nose twitch. It was bad enough that Patrick hadn't confided in her about his real plans. And it was possible that someone else was interested in the *Noble*'s cargo. But everything Sophie had shared with them shrunk in comparison to one simple truth.

Her dad had broken his promise to her. A promise he'd kept since she was fourteen years old when he told her that he'd always be there for her. That he wouldn't do anything to put himself at risk…like her mother had.

"What do you mean you can't get in touch with them?" Sam paced the length of the telephone cord and reversed direction when he reached the end of it. He lowered his voice, aware of Evie and Sophie in the next room and Faith asleep on the couch several yards away. "What if there's an emergency?"

"Our pilot flies into the camps once a week with

supplies," the proprietor of the lodge informed him. "Even in an emergency, the earliest we could get a message to your father would be next Monday or Tuesday."

Not good enough. Sam had to warn Patrick what had happened to Evie and find out who else was interested in the *Noble*. He already had a strong hunch *why* they were interested. Legends of sunken treasure lured hundreds of divers to the Great Lakes. Even though Sophie was right about laws existing to protect areas designated underwater preserves, there were unscrupulous people willing to break them.

Bruce Mullins, if he remembered correctly, had served in the Marines with his father. Maybe all he'd done was mention the *Noble* to a relative or friend he thought he could trust and it had sparked their interest.

But how had Seth Lansky zeroed in on Patrick's computer files instead of going to Sophie—the source of the information?

"Mr. Cutter? Are you still there? What is the message you'd like me to deliver?"

"Ah…could you tell the pilot to have him call home as soon as possible?"

Silence.

Sam rolled his eyes at the ceiling. Right. *Phone home.* That sounded like a legitimate reason to send a pilot on an unscheduled flight to an isolated fishing camp.

"I'll pass the message on, Mr. Cutter. Was there anything else?" Her tone made it clear she hoped not.

"No. Thank you." Sam hung up the phone.

The grandfather clock in the corner of the room came to life. Ten o'clock. The past few hours had disappeared, absorbed by Sophie's story about her family and Matthew Graham. Under any other circumstances, Sam would have been fascinated. But not now. Not with Jacob and Patrick out of reach and Evie alone at the house.

Another wave of helplessness rolled over him. He'd come to the Upper Peninsula to take a break from his problems, not add to them. But Patrick had called him. Warned him that Evie might be in danger and asked him to look out for her.

He couldn't leave her unprotected, especially if whoever was interested in the ship was convinced Patrick's computer files held the key to the *Noble* and her secrets.

Hopefully the incident with Lansky would prevent Evie from giving another stranger access to her home, but anyone could show up at Beach Glass during the day, pretending to be a customer.

As much as he wanted Evie to continue tutoring Faith, he didn't want to risk Evie's safety. When he'd pulled her to the ground so Seth wouldn't see them, her slender body had stiffened in his arms, tight as a bowstring. She was fragile. Vulnerable. There was only one thing to do. Convince her to pack her bags, close up shop and go home. And it probably wouldn't take much convincing. She was such a cautious little thing….

Decision made, Sam padded into the sitting room and saw the two women sitting shoulder to shoulder on the old settee. Hands clasped. Heads bowed.

Praying?

He paused in the doorway, feeling like an intruder, as Evie's soft voice filled the quiet.

"…and heavenly Father, we turn to you for strength. And for wisdom. Protect the people we love and bring them safely home. For now, we trust they are in Your care."

The words sailed through the empty places in his heart. What was it like to be so sure Someone was listening? Someone who really had the power to give strength? Over the past few months, his had drained away. Punctured by the bullet wounds in his brother's spine. Dan had always come to him for advice. But now, when Dan needed him the most, Sam found he had nothing. Nothing to give. Nothing to say. Nothing that could reverse the clock or give his brother hope for the future.

Dan hated him for it.

And Sam hated himself.

Chapter Nine

Evie lifted her head and saw Sam standing in the doorway. The raw pain in his eyes burned its way through her before the shutters slammed back into place.

"I can't get through to them until next week," he said flatly. "Bruce Mullins took them to one of the more isolated camps."

Evie felt a flash of hope. "So they did go fishing?"

"I doubt it." Sam stalked into the room. "Maybe you should stay with Sophie tonight."

He still thought she was in danger.

Evie wavered, remembering the way Seth Lansky's massive paw had circled her wrist. Had he given up or was there a chance he might come back?

You will keep in perfect peace him whose mind is steadfast, because he trusts in you.

The verse from Isaiah that Sophie had quoted

while they'd prayed cycled back through Evie's mind. Peace followed trust. That's what she had to remember. "I need to go home. Dad might call again and he'll want to know I'm all right."

"If we can't contact them, they won't be able to contact us," Sam pointed out.

"I have plenty of room," Sophie added, concern for Evie evident in the slight furrow between her eyebrows. "Tyson reclaimed his old room upstairs, but the sofa in the living room pulls out into a bed."

Evie had forgotten about Tyson. Even though he was Sophie's son, something about the guy creeped her out. "I appreciate the invitation, Sophie, but I still have to open Beach Glass in the morning. I'll be fine. I think Sam spooked Seth Lansky enough that he won't be coming back."

The thought occurred to her that maybe that was why Seth had boldly talked his way into the house. With Patrick gone, he'd assumed she was alone. Vulnerable.

"Can you take me home, Sam?" Evie ignored the hollow pit in her stomach at the thought of going back to the isolated house again. "I know you and Faith are going out on the boat tomorrow morning. She needs a good night's sleep."

I'll keep my mind on You, Lord, and trust You to provide the peace.

"Let me know the second you hear from Patrick and Jacob." Sophie's eyes clouded over. "I wish now that I'd never gotten them involved in this."

"It's not your fault," Evie murmured, unable to resist a pointed look at Sam.

"Once Patrick found out what I was doing, he begged me to let him help," Sophie continued. "That man does love a challenge."

"You mean Jacob," Evie corrected her gently.

"No. Patrick." A smile played at the corners of Sophie's lips. "I think he would have bought a wet suit and gone diving for the *Noble* himself if Jacob hadn't convinced him to contact Bruce Mullins first."

"Good old Dad. The voice of reason." Sam arched an eyebrow at Evie.

They *couldn't* be talking about Patrick McBride. The most challenging thing her dad tackled was the expert-level crossword puzzle book she bought him for his birthday every year!

The car's headlights barely made a dent in the darkness as Sam drove her home. Sophie had insisted he allow Faith to spend the night, and as Evie stared out the window at the thick stands of trees hemming the edge of the road, she wished she'd taken advantage of the offer now, too.

"Do you think Dad is in trouble?" Evie finally voiced the question churning in her mind since they'd left Sophie's.

"They're with an experienced guide," Sam said. "I'm sure they're fine."

Was it her imagination, or had he put the slightest emphasis on the word *they're?*

"I still can't believe Dad is involved in this," Evie murmured. "Helping Sophie is one thing but traipsing around, looking for a ship that may not even exist is totally out of character for him. And we have no idea who this Seth Lansky is. Or what he was trying to find."

"That's why you should go home."

Evie's mouth dropped open as the quiet force of the words vibrated in the silence. "Go home?"

"There's a real possibility you aren't safe here. Someone else is interested in the *Noble,* and they knew exactly who to go to for information. Patrick said you might be in danger. He would expect you to leave. Close up Beach Glass until I can make contact with them again and sort out this mess."

It was so tempting to grab hold of the suggestion. To put miles between her and whatever threat lurked around the corner. Would her dad want her to turn tail and run away?

You don't have to be here to talk to Dad, a logical voice in her head reminded her. *You can be at home just as easily.*

"The tourist season is just getting started," Sam continued in that calm, reasonable tone. "Even if you closed up the antique shop for a week, you wouldn't lose much business."

"I'm staying."

The announcement stunned Evie almost as much as Sam.

"There's no guarantee that you're safe," he said flatly.

Funny how those simple words shook her to the core. All her life, Evie had chosen *safe*. She'd built her life around it. Hadn't she learned that people who deliberately put themselves in dangerous situations eventually paid too high of a price? And so did the people they loved.

But what if her dad returned unexpectedly? Shouldn't she be waiting for him? And what about Faith? If God had brought them together, Evie had to trust she was under His protection and He'd give her the strength she needed.

"God brought me here for a reason," Evie said through dry lips. "I'm not leaving."

Sam didn't try to change her mind, but Evie had the feeling he wasn't happy she was staying. Or with the reason why.

"Hi, Evie."

At the unexpected greeting, Evie almost dropped the Depression-glass sugar bowl cradled in her hands.

"Faith." Evie looked at her in surprise before glancing at the row of whimsical cuckoo clocks mounted on the wall. Three o'clock. "Did you and Sam come in early today?"

Faith's face closed, reminding her of Sam's expression when he'd caught her and Sophie praying the night before. "Sam didn't want to take the boat out. It's supposed to storm later this afternoon."

The robin's-egg-blue sky, decorated with brush-strokes of wispy clouds, didn't look the least bit threatening at the moment, but Evie was glad Sam had chosen to believe the weather forecast over the clear sky.

"Is Sam with you?"

"Uh-uh." Suddenly, Faith became fascinated with the canning jar next to the old-fashioned cash register on the counter.

Warning bells went off in Evie's head. "Faith, does he know you're here?"

"What's this?" Faith avoided the question, studying the contents of the jar on the counter as if she'd never seen anything like it before.

"It's beach glass." Evie gave the girl an exasper-ated smile. Science lesson or lecture? She decided there was time for both. "The waves and the sand work together like a rock tumbler until the glass is smooth and polished."

"Cool."

Evie smiled. One word that equaled high praise. "Go ahead and take one. Dad won't mind. Banks give out Tootsie Rolls, and Dad gives out pieces of beach glass. He says they last longer."

As soon as her thoughts returned to her dad, worry scurried back, chewing at Evie's peace of mind like a nest of field mice. She'd managed to keep her fear under control throughout the long night and most of the morning, but there were times it snuck up on her. Like right now.

"Look at this one. It looks like a piece of bubble-gum." Faith held up a piece of glass in a shade of deep pink and for the first time, Evie noticed the girl's red-rimmed eyes and the faint pleats at the corners of her lips. "Pink is Mom's favorite color. Every Christmas, Dad buys her something pink even though he says it's a girlie color. He bought me a pink baseball mitt as a joke for my birthday once."

Faith bravely cracked open the door to her heart to see if Evie really cared about what was inside. She did. But now she had to convince her.

God, please give me the right words to say.

"Have you talked to your Dad lately?"

"When I called this morning, Mom said he was asleep."

The uncertainty in Faith's voice told Evie she didn't know if she should believe her.

"You must miss him a lot."

"I do." Faith dropped the piece of glass back into the jar. "But I heard Mom tell Sam that Dad isn't the same person anymore. Maybe...he doesn't miss me."

Evie drew in a careful breath, but it still felt like a knife sliding between her ribs. Obviously Faith had listened in on a conversation not meant for her ears. No one had been honest with Faith about her father's situation, and while Evie understood that her family thought they were protecting her, it had forced Faith to try to make sense of it on her own. And without wisdom and experience to temper her thoughts, Faith had come to the wrong conclusion.

"I'm sure your dad misses you very much," she contradicted softly. "But he has to accept some major changes in his life and that isn't easy. It isn't easy for anyone."

"I want things to be the way they were," Faith admitted in a small voice.

"They won't be the same." Evie knew she had to be honest. "But that doesn't mean they can't be better." She retrieved the piece of glass and held it on her open palm. "Look at this. It's still a piece of glass, right? But it's changed. At one point in time, it would have been sharp enough to cut you. But the waves and the sand gradually rounded the edges. Softened it. I'm praying for your dad, Faith. That he'll open his heart and trust that God is big enough to bring something good out of this situation."

She wrapped her arm around Faith's shoulders and felt them stiffen. And then Faith melted against her.

"I'll pray, too."

"Good girl," Evie murmured. "Now, how about I call your uncle, who's probably tearing apart the forest looking for you, and tell him we're going to have school earlier today?"

"Field trip?" Faith smiled hopefully.

"English first. Then maybe we can fit in a short field trip."

"Look at this." Faith squatted down and pulled a chunk of rock out of the ground.

"It's quartz." Evie stooped down to admire her find and smiled when she saw Faith's bulging pockets. The girl already had a good start on a rock collection. Evie's own pockets were full, a testimony to the fact she had a difficult time passing up interesting rocks, too.

"I'll give it to Sam for his desk. Then he'll see it every day."

"He spends a lot of time in an office?" The words rolled out before Evie could stop them, and she winced. Talk about blatant curiosity! Faith, thank goodness, didn't think there was anything unusual about the question.

"Dad always teases him about being a paper pusher or something." Faith rubbed the rock against the hem of her T-shirt and left a trail of grime on the fabric.

Evie wasn't surprised at Faith's affirmation that Sam worked in some kind of corporate setting. And she couldn't help feeling a little relieved, although she didn't want to examine *that* too closely.

When he'd left the night before, he hadn't been happy with her decision to stay in Cooper's Landing, and he'd made it clear he thought she was making a huge mistake.

It isn't as if you've shown a lot of backbone up to this point, Evie admitted to herself. She'd shaken like an aspen leaf when she'd seen that diving equipment in the back of Seth's van. No wonder Sam worried about her being alone. Some witness for God she was turning out to be. If Sam looked at her as an example of a believer, he'd think they were a bunch of wimps!

A raindrop splashed on the back of Evie's wrist. When she looked up, the blue sky had all but disappeared, filled with a slow-moving armada of dark cumulus clouds.

"Faith, let's get going. It looks like the storm that kept you off the lake is finally moving in."

A shard of lightning and a low growl of thunder in the distance underscored the point. Evie silently chided herself for being so focused on the ground that she hadn't paid attention to what was over their heads!

"We're going to get wet," Faith predicted.

Probably an understatement, Evie thought. *Soaked* was more like it. They had at least a two-mile hike back to the house. The beauty of the woods had enchanted them, luring them farther down the trail than Evie had originally planned.

She dug in her purse and pulled out her compact umbrella, popping it open and holding it over Faith's head. "Let's try this."

Faith grinned up at her. "You remind me of Mary

Poppins. Remember, she had that great big carpet-bag with a mirror in it? And a lamp?"

"I remember," Evie muttered as a gust of wind caught the umbrella and turned it inside out. "If I were Mary Poppins, my umbrella would behave."

They dashed down the trail as the light sprinkles, which must have been the opening preshow, became a pelting rain.

At one point, Faith slipped and fell. Rocks tumbled out of her pockets and she scrambled to gather them up again.

Evie quickly doubled back. "Don't worry, Faith. We can find more."

"I can't find the one I was going to give Sam." Faith had to raise her voice above the sudden screech of the wind.

Evie scooped a handful of soggy hair out of her eyes so she could aid in the search. "Look. Here it is." Rivulets of muddy water coasted down her arm when she picked it up. Soaked *and* dirty. With a new story to tell her students in the fall.

Faith cocked her head, reminding Evie of Sophie's puppies. "I hear a car. Maybe Sam is looking for us."

Evie heard it, too. For a brief moment, hope burst inside her. Until she remembered. "The gate was locked. It has to be a government vehicle of some kind."

"Maybe they can give us a ride!" Faith whooped and sprinted into the woods separating the service road from the trail.

Through the trees, Evie caught a glimpse of a white van creeping along the road.

It couldn't be.

"Faith! Wait." Evie was no track star but the rush of adrenaline rocketing through her blood pushed her into high gear. She caught up to Faith just before the girl stepped into the road.

"Hey!" Faith squawked in protest as Evie pulled her down behind a clump of foliage.

"It's not a government vehicle." Evie tucked Faith tightly against her as the van rolled past them, so close she could have reached out and touched the tire. A shiver ripped through her as she read the license plate, which bore the same number she'd seen on the one parked in her driveway.

Seth Lansky.

Was he looking for her?

Evie bit her lip, thinking quickly. If Seth really was following them, he probably thought they'd gone to the scenic overlook. That meant she and Faith had a chance to make it back to the parking area before Seth realized they weren't where he thought they'd be.

Thank you, God, for watching out for us.

And bless Faith and her adventurous spirit.

If they'd stuck to the service road, Seth would have spotted them immediately. Not that he'd pursue them on foot...

Out of the corner of her eye, Evie saw the red

glow of the brake lights and watched as the driver nosed the vehicle into a narrow clearing.

He was turning around.

"Come on." Evie caught hold of Faith's hand and pulled her back toward the trail, their progress hampered by the brush dragging at their clothing and a grid of exposed tree roots that stretched out like a minefield beneath their feet.

"Evie, you're scaring me." Faith vaulted over a fallen log and clutched Evie's arm as she slipped on a slick bed of decaying leaves. "Who is that?"

"I'm not sure." It was the truth. Evie had no idea if the man driving the van was Seth Lansky...but it couldn't be a coincidence the three of them had wound up in the woods together at the same time.

The wind swallowed Faith's shriek as a shard of lightning hurtled out of the sky, incinerating a nearby tree. The ground trembled under their feet. Evie trembled, too, but didn't want Faith to know she was afraid.

"Not too much farther, Faith. You can do it."

Through the sheet of water cascading over the brim of her hat, Evie saw the gate up ahead. As they veered around it, she tripped over something. The heavy padlock that secured the gate to the post lay on the ground. Clipped off by something a little sturdier than a pair of pliers.

"I see the restrooms," Faith gasped.

Evie gave the girl's arm a reassuring squeeze.

Tourists would be in the parking lot, waiting for the rain to subside. And Seth Lansky wouldn't dare approach them in front of witnesses.

Just as the terrain changed from dirt to concrete beneath their feet, Evie heard the faint, muffled purr of an engine. Fear seared her lungs and she scanned the parking lot.

Empty.

Chapter Ten

Evie stopped, bending over to massage the stitch in her side. Should they stay on the trail and try to make it home or take refuge in the restroom? Maybe Seth had checked them already and wouldn't bother a second time.

She had about thirty seconds to decide before Seth spotted them in the parking lot. Evie's gaze darted to the trail and gauged the distance. A straight shot fifty yards in before it took a slight turn that would conceal them from sight.

They didn't have time.

"Restroom," Evie decided, lurching toward the tiny building. Faith remained close at her heels and they skidded inside just as the van rattled around the gate.

Evie collapsed against the wall and Faith slumped to the floor beside her. Outside, the van's engine idled in harmony with their ragged breathing.

Keep going, Evie silently urged the driver. It's pouring. You don't want to go out in this storm.

The snick of a car door closing sounded more ominous than the crack of lightning that had demolished the top of a tree.

"You don't happen to have a phone booth in your purse, do you?" Faith hopped to her feet.

The complete look of trust in the girl's eyes stunned Evie. And goaded her into action.

"We don't need a phone booth. We need a distraction."

Think, Evie.

The restroom had been equipped with the bare essentials. Paper towel holder. A soap dispenser on the wall. And a locked cabinet under the sink.

Bingo.

"Faith, there's a package of gum in my purse. Unwrap all the sticks and give me the foil." Faith looked at her as if she'd lost her mind and Evie managed a quick smile. "Trust me. I'm a science teacher."

While Faith tackled her assignment, Evie peeled off the cabinet hinges with the miniature screwdriver on her Swiss Army knife. Fear made her clumsy and she forced herself to take a deep, calming breath, praying the contents of the cabinet would yield what she needed.

"Here you go," Faith whispered.

Evie closed her eyes in relief when she saw the old

bottle of drain cleaner stashed in the back of the cabinet with the rest of the cleaning supplies.

"Now I need you to look in the garbage for a large plastic soda bottle. Find one with a lid."

Faith wrinkled her nose but obeyed.

Evie licked her lips. Now came the hard part. She had to spot Seth before he spotted them.

"Faith, we're going to get out of here but we can't go home yet. There are some rustic cabins the Forest Service rents out on Porcupine Trail. Did you see them on the map?" At Faith's tentative nod, Evie patted her knee. "Good girl. We're going to head there and wait out the storm in one of them."

Hopefully by now, Sam would be looking for them, too.

Evie crept to the door and peered out. No one sat in the driver's seat of the van. Where was he? Evie edged out a little more and caught a glimpse of Seth's bulky frame near the trail. He had his back to them.

"When I give you the signal, head down the trail to the left."

"You're leaving me?" Panic flared in Faith's eyes.

"I'll be right behind you. I promise."

Faith's head bobbed. "What's the signal?"

"You'll know it when you hear it."

Evie filled the bottle with drain cleaner, shoved the foil into her pocket and sprinted toward the van. Seth had melted farther into the woods, and Evie knew she had only precious seconds before he realized they hadn't gone that way. Now she had no doubt he'd check the restrooms again.

Just as she skidded around the side of the vehicle, Seth appeared, lumbering back up the trail and heading straight for the restroom where Faith waited.

She shoved the foil wrappers into the bottle, screwed the lid back on, eased the door to the van open and lobbed it inside like a grenade.

Thank you Brian and Tyler for your science fair experiment. Let's hope it works on a smaller scale.

Evie made it to the woods just as an explosion burst over the sound of the rain.

Seth's startled bellow told her it had.

The chill settling in Sam's bones had nothing to do with the sudden drop in temperature as two weather systems collided in the heavens above him.

Evie and Faith were nowhere to be found. The front door of the shop had been locked up tight. So had the house. Which could only mean one thing—Evie and Faith had taken another unscheduled field trip.

Sam's back teeth ground together. "I can't look out for you when you disappear on me, Evie."

The rain sheeted the car windows and lightning still backlit the clouds, accompanied by the low rumble of thunder. Hopefully, they'd taken shelter somewhere until the storm passed. Sam didn't want to consider the alternative.

"This is crazy." Sam twisted around, searching

the backseat of the car for a discarded hat or jacket. Anything to prevent an immediate soaking when he got out of the car. The only thing his search yielded was the crumpled copy of *Captain's Courageous* from Faith's summer reading list, a candy wrapper and a lime-green baseball cap. Way too small and not his color.

Evie's car was still parked by the garage, which meant they'd taken off on foot. If they'd stayed close to home, the storm would have pushed them back to the house by now.

Sam exhaled in frustration, wishing he knew the area better. He rifled through the glove compartment, remembering he'd shoved a bunch of tourist brochures into it on the drive up. A minuscule map showed a series of hiking trails less than three miles from Beach Glass.

Three miles. Judging from the map, he could drive in only as far as the rest area and then he'd have to hoof it from there. But he had to start somewhere. He wasn't a person who got rattled easily, but he'd feel a lot better knowing Evie and Faith were safe and sound. So he could chew them out for worrying him.

"What *was* that?" Faith's eyes were wide as Evie caught up to her on the trail.

"Just a little something I learned from the boys in my class."

"It sounded like a bomb."

"No, making homemade bombs is irresponsible. Reckless. I made a *distraction,* remember?"

"It was a good one."

"Thank you." The muscles in Evie's stomach cramped again, and she decided two miles a day on the treadmill didn't prepare a girl for running for cover over uneven terrain. "If my calculations are right, one of the cabins should be to the west of us about half a mile."

Rustic campsite didn't quite describe what they found at the end of the path, but at least it was a roof over their heads. Sort of. A one-room cabin fashioned from weathered cedar, equipped with screens instead of windows. A single bedframe complete with a questionable foam mattress. A fireplace layered with a thick coat of ash and a plank floor covered with droppings.

"Myotis lucifugus," Evie murmured.

"What's that?" Faith asked nervously.

"A bat." Evie scanned the ceiling to see if the culprit was still in residence. "Don't worry. All clear."

"I'm kind of c-c-cold." Faith wrapped her arms around her middle and perched gingerly on the edge of the bed.

Now that they'd managed to shake Seth loose, Evie had to concentrate on getting them dry. She rummaged in her bag and handed Faith a chocolate-dipped granola bar. "Here. Eat this. I'll try to start a fire." If she could find some dry kindling.

Faith read her mind. "We don't have any wood."

Evie poked at the ashes in the fireplace and turned up several chunks of charred embers. She wove her fingers together and closed her eyes.

"What are you doing? Did you get something in your eye?" Faith leaned forward.

Evie shook her head. "I was asking God for help."

"Starting a fire?"

"Of course. Have you ever heard the story of the loaves and fishes?"

Faith shook her head. "No."

"It's in the Bible. A huge crowd gathered all day to listen to Jesus talk. His friends told him to send the people away because everyone was hungry. Jesus asked what they had and all they could come up with was a few loaves of bread and some fish. Jesus blessed it and when his friends passed it out, those little loaves and fishes fed over five thousand people."

"Is that true?" Faith asked doubtfully.

"Yes, it is. And I'll tell you something else that's true. God cares about the small details of our lives as much as He cares about the big ones. I have the matches and few sticks and we'll let God handle the fire." She struck a match and held it against a splinter of charred wood, then blew carefully until a lick of flame chased up the length of it.

Another rumble of thunder rolled above them like a freight car, rattling the screens on the cabin.

"Look, Evie!" Faith stared in awe at the smoke

curling into the air, born from the tiny flame that had begun to devour one of the chunks of wood.

"I'm going outside to make sure that smoke is going up the chimney like it's supposed to." Evie stood up and felt water squish in her shoes with every step.

Wisps of smoke emerged from the chimney, and Evie's gaze carefully moved from tree to tree. Maybe the heavy rain was a blessing in disguise. Seth didn't seem like the type of guy who carried an umbrella.

She eased back into the cabin and found Faith on her knees in front of the fireplace, hands splayed over the flames.

"Are we going to stay here for a while?"

Good question. And one Evie didn't have an answer to yet. She'd tucked some snacks into her bag before they'd set out but didn't normally carry a change of clothing! And both of them were soaked to the skin.

"Just until the rain subsides. Not that we can get any wetter."

Faith's eyes clouded. "Sam is going to be mad."

"He might be worried, but he won't be mad."

"It looks the same," Faith responded glumly.

"You might be right about that." Evie hid a smile. In spite of his annoying tendency to boss people around, Evie didn't doubt Sam's love for his niece. Not many men would take time off from work to care for a troubled adolescent, family or not.

"No one tells me anything." Faith stared into the

fire, a frown puckering her brow. "I wanted to stay with Dad, but they didn't give me a choice. They made me come here."

They. It explained the tension between Faith and Sam. She blamed him for taking her away from her father. Evie didn't understand why Dan Cutter's family hadn't stayed to cheer him on during his recovery, either, but everyone had a different way of dealing with crises.

"Sometimes parents make decisions we don't understand," Evie said slowly. "But it's because they love us and want to protect us."

Faith's shoulders rolled in time with her heavy sigh. "So your mom did that, too? Did it drive you crazy?"

Laura McBride's face pieced together in Evie's memory like a tattered photograph. Her mother had loved her family but had chosen to protect everyone else. And where had that left Evie and her sisters?

"All moms do." Evie chose the safest response.

In a rapid change of moods, a mischievous sparkle lit Faith's eyes. "We need more loaves and fishes." She poked at the fire with a stick and it flared back to life. "Dry ones."

Evie doubted she could find a dry stick in the forest at the moment, but the steady drum of the rain against the roof had quieted. "It doesn't seem to be raining as hard anymore. We should be able to leave soon."

"Do you think *he's* still there? The man you didn't want to see us?"

"I don't know." Fear pinched Evie again as she imagined the long trek back to the house. And the very real possibility that Seth was still out there somewhere, waiting for them. His deliberate search for her brought back a rush of doubts. Maybe retreat was the best option. She didn't want to put Faith in danger.

Maybe you should go home.

"Maybe you should pray," Faith said simply.

"Thanks for the reminder." Evie choked back a laugh. Out of the mouths of babes! "Don't get too close to the fire. I'm going outside to check the chimney again." A flimsy excuse, but she couldn't tell Faith she planned to sneak up the trail and make sure it was safe to leave.

The storm had exhausted its power, and Evie saw patches of blue sky through the trees as she picked her way cautiously down the trail. What she wouldn't give for a hot shower and a cup of tea...

The crack of a branch turned her knees to water. Not more than fifty yards off the trail, a man moved purposefully in the direction of the cabin.

Seth?

Evie ducked behind the thick trunk of a white pine. Even above the sound of the rain, Evie was sure her ragged gasps of breath would give her away. Somehow, she had to get to the cabin before he did. Or, Evie thought with a flash of inspiration, draw him *away* from it.

Dropping to her knees, Evie scooted around the

tree. "Okay, Big Guy. Let's see what you've got...." The words died as she found herself face-to-knees with the man towering over her.

He hauled Evie to her feet so quickly she barely had time to process the long legs encased in blue jeans, black sweatshirt stretched over a broad, muscular chest. And a soggy, lime-green baseball cap.

Eyes as gray as the storm clouds captured hers.

For one heart-stopping moment, Sam pulled her against him, his fingers combing through her tangled hair with gentle roughness. And then he let her go.

"I've got trouble, that's what I've got," Sam said softly. "It's about five foot five with red hair, blue eyes and a habit of taking unscheduled field trips."

Chapter Eleven

"A man was looking for us," Faith announced from the backseat of the car.

Sam's foot pumped the accelerator, spewing gravel off the back tires. Neither Evie nor Faith had said much on the trek back to the parking lot, and he'd assumed they'd taken refuge in the little cabin to wait out the storm. Until now. "What man?"

"A man in a white van. But Evie made a—"

"*Distraction*," Evie interrupted, shifting on the seat beside him.

"Uh-huh. A distraction." Faith nodded vigorously in agreement.

A white van. Seth Lansky again. Which could only mean one thing. He must have decided that since he couldn't get into Patrick's computer, he'd set his sights on the next logical source of information. Evie.

Sam had given in to her stubborn insistence to

stay in Cooper's Landing once, but he wouldn't do it again. Not when Patrick had asked him to watch out for her. Evie had eluded Seth this time, but there was no guarantee she could do so again. Lansky might not be a physical threat, but Sam wasn't willing to take a chance.

"I'll drop Faith off to change clothes first and then I'll take you home." To make sure you pack your bags.

Evie didn't argue. Sam slanted a look at her, feeling an unfamiliar tug of *something* when he noticed the weary slump of her shoulders and the damp copper hair plastered against the nape of her neck. Hair he'd untangled with his fingers.

Sam's hands tightened on the steering wheel. He had no excuse for that. Maybe it was somehow connected to the relief that had slammed into his gut when he'd seen Evie scurry behind a tree near one of the Forest Service cabins. She'd looked as stunned by his unexpected embrace as he was. Immediately, he'd put some distance between them but that hadn't doused the confusing mix of emotions Evie always seemed to dredge up in him. And life was confusing enough at the moment, thanks, so now he planned to brush up on his grammar skills, take over as Faith's tutor and send Evie packing. For her own good. And maybe, Sam admitted, for *his*.

By the time they pulled up to the cabin, the sun was shining bravely again, gifting them with a spectacular double rainbow.

Faith propped her arms on the back of Evie's seat and gave them an engaging grin. "A rainbow is formed by the refraction and reflection of the sun's rays in the raindrops, right?"

Evie smiled. "That's true, but the Bible says it's also God's promise never to destroy the world with water again."

"Really?" Faith blinked. "That's in the Bible? Like the story of the loaves and fishes?"

Sam felt Evie's questioning glance and hot color crept into his face. The Cutters tended to live by the old Pull Yourselves Up By The Bootstraps motto. All his life, Jacob had impressed upon his sons that they had everything in them necessary for life. Courage. Strength. Discipline. All they had to do was mine it out and use it. If they didn't, they had no one to blame but themselves. Asking for help from an unseen God was never offered as an option. The closest Sam got to Him was at Thanksgiving, when they bowed their heads and offered a weak prayer of thanks under Grandma Cutter's watchful eye.

When Sam had walked in on Evie and Sophie praying the night before, he'd felt something stir the emptiness inside and wondered if it was too late to approach God. And if it was a sign of weakness.

Jacob would think so. When a friend of Rachel's had asked the pastor of her church to visit Dan, Jacob had intercepted the man and politely told him to tend to his own "flock" and he would see to his.

The image of Dan, confined to a hospital bed, sawed through Sam again like the serrated edge of a knife. His brother's career and favorite hobbies required the use of his legs. He could still see the hopeless look in Dan's eyes. Even his wife and daughter failed to move him toward recovery. And instead of being encouraging, Jacob's admonitions to Dan—that if he set his mind on recovery, he'd be walking in no time—had only made Dan pull further into himself.

"Do you have a Bible, Sam?" Faith asked.

"No." The word came out more harshly than he intended.

"I'm sure Dad has an extra one. I'd be happy to let you borrow it, Faith," Evie said carefully.

Faith looked at him expectantly, and Sam decided that even though it might not help, it probably couldn't hurt, either. "I'm okay with it." He hoped the rest of his family would be, too.

"As long as you don't test me on it." Faith giggled.

"I make no promises." Evie turned back to Sam. "I'll wait here in the car while you get Faith settled."

"We've got towels inside. You should at least come in and dry your hair." Sam saw the blush that rose in Evie's cheeks as she glanced away. Strange. Evie wasn't exactly shy. The night he'd urged her to pretend they'd been on a romantic stroll, her fluttering lashes and adoring look had convinced Seth they were a couple. Just when his cynical self decided he was seeing an unexpected side of Evie McBride, she'd struggled to come up with an appropriate endearment. *Dear.* His lips twisted at the memory. Straight from a rerun of *Happy Days*.

As Sam followed Evie up the path to the cabin, he found himself wondering if there was someone special in her life. Jacob had mentioned all of Patrick's daughters were single, but that didn't mean Evie didn't have a significant other. Someone who could overlook her exasperating tendency to preplan every step and carry a bag guaranteed to make a tinker jealous…and who would appreciate the sapphire-blue eyes that could take a man down like one of the hapless ships at the bottom of the lake.

Where had that come from?

Sam's heart locked up. No, thanks. Been there, done that, had the scars to prove it.

He'd been engaged at the ripe old age of twenty-five to a woman who'd confronted him a week before the wedding, asking him to choose between her and his career. He must have hesitated a fraction of a second too long because Kelly had walked out the door, taking the choice away from him.

Some deep soul-searching and a game of one-on-one with Dan at midnight had left him with a broken finger, a bloody nose and the conclusion he wasn't the marrying kind. Lucky for him that Dan was. Sam could focus on his career with the added bonus of hanging out with his brother's family unit several times a month, enjoying home-cooked meals from Rachel's kitchen and the chance to be Faith's doting uncle without having to change diapers or do that burping thing.

After a week in Faith's company, he'd begun to think diapers and walking around with a towel tossed over his shoulder to catch whatever didn't stay down had been easier than the stage she was in now. Earlier in the day he'd caught her on the phone, trying to sweet-talk the receptionist into letting her talk to Dan. The woman had refused to put the call through, but for some reason Faith had blamed *him*. And then she'd taken off. He'd been about to go to Sophie's when Evie had called him to let him know Faith was with her.

Sam felt a pang of regret. Faith wasn't going to be happy when she found out Evie was leaving. Hopefully, he could make her understand.

Right. Like she understood when you took her away from her dad and brought her here.

Sam pushed the thought aside, more comfortable with action than feelings. "Faith, get some dry towels for Evie, too, okay?"

"Okay." Faith disappeared up the stairs to the loft, leaving them alone.

"I'll stay here. I don't want to drip on the hardwood f-floors."

The faint chatter of Evie's teeth reminded Sam that she'd been soaked to the skin for several hours.

"I'll be right back." He disappeared into the bedroom and came back with a pair of clean sweatpants and a long-sleeved T-shirt. "Here. The bathroom is down the hall on the left."

Evie balked. "You're t-taking me home, right? I'll be fine for a few more minutes."

"Just wear them and put me out of your misery," Sam told her curtly.

A smile danced in Evie's eyes. "Now I *know* I look as horrible as I feel."

Horrible? Not the word Sam would have chosen. With her wide blue eyes and tousled hair, she reminded him of a stray kitten who'd been left out in the rain. "At least you don't look like a raccoon."

"Th-thanks."

She looked confused, so Sam figured he should clarify. "You don't have those dark runny circles under your eyes."

Her laughter reminded him of the wind chimes on the deck. "Those are from mascara. And I gave up on makeup when I realized *nothing* hides f-freckles."

Sam frowned as another shiver rippled through her. "I'll change while you put these on, and then I'll give you a ride home."

"He's bossy, isn't he, Evie?" Faith called from the loft as she leaned over the railing and dropped two colorful beach towels.

"You're insulting me?" Sam couldn't believe it. "The guy who rescued you this afternoon?"

Faith gave him an impish grin. "I think Evie's *bomb* rescued us."

"Bomb?" Sam narrowed his gaze on Evie, who shrugged.

"Actually…it was a *distraction*." Plucking the clothes out of Sam's hands, Evie scooted down the hall to the bathroom. She knew what was coming next. He was going to try to talk her into leaving. Again.

She turned the lock and sagged against the door, unsure whether her bones were rattling because the storm had turned her into a walking sponge or in a delayed reaction to their close call with Seth.

Hands shaking, she managed to strip off her wet clothes. As she tugged the well-laundered T-shirt over her head, the familiar blend of soap, fresh air and forest teased her nose. She buried her face in the crook of her elbow and inhaled, comforted by the scent. Sam's scent. It was strange how they barely knew each other, yet she recognized it so quickly.

The black sweatpants puddled around her feet, but at least they were dry. Evie rolled up the bottoms three times and decided it was the best she could do. But when she saw her reflection in the mirror, she stifled a groan. Maybe she didn't look like a raccoon, but Sam had neglected to mention she looked like a drowned rat! Her hair sprang every which way and there were faint scratches on her forehead from being attacked by a low-hanging branch.

When she emerged from the bathroom a few

minutes later, she found a drowsy Faith curled up on the couch, headphones in place and a cup of hot chocolate cradled in her palms. She yawned and pointed to the kitchen.

Sam stood at the breakfast counter, slathering peanut butter on a piece of bread. "Coffee or hot chocolate? No tea in this house. Dad doesn't think it's manly."

Evie hooked her thumbs in the waistband of the sweatpants and hiked them up as she sidled into the kitchen. "Coffee. Please."

Sam turned and his gaze swept over her. A smile twisted his lips. "I should have given you something of Faith's to wear."

"This is fine. Thank you." Evie pushed the words out, self-conscious under the weight of his quiet appraisal.

"Foil and drain cleaner," Sam murmured, padding over to her and handing her the peanut butter sandwich she'd assumed was for Faith.

Faith had taken advantage of her absence and spilled the beans. "Seth was about to search the restrooms and Faith was trapped inside. I had to do something to distract him so she could get away."

"Very ingenious." Sam's eyes warmed to liquid silver. "The woman has brains…and beauty."

Beauty? Evie instantly rejected the notion. Caitlin and Meghan reigned as the unchallenged beauties of the McBride family. Caitlin's classic features, sable dark hair and pale blue eyes may have contrasted with Meghan's exotic green eyes and untamed straw-berry-blond curls, but both women drew their share of appreciative glances.

Her sisters, only two years apart in age, had been the darlings of Abraham Lincoln High School. The phone had rung off the hook on the weekends. Boys called to take her sisters to a movie or out for a burger. They called Evie when they needed a lab partner.

Sam was probably used to dropping compliments. The night they'd fooled Seth into believing they were a couple, he'd turned on the charm without missing a beat. And his rakish good looks and easy confidence guaranteed a watercooler fan club out there somewhere. He was a man comfortable in his own skin, something Evie had never quite mastered. Old insecurities seemed to hang on like a piece of tape stuck to the bottom of her shoe.

It was a depressing thought.

"I want to go home." Evie closed her eyes as a wave of fatigue swamped her. She didn't deserve any praise. Not when all she'd done was help Faith escape from the dangerous situation she'd put her into to begin with.

"Sit down and eat the sandwich." Sam didn't wait for her to comply, just took her by the elbows and steered her toward the kitchen table. "You look like you're ready to fall over."

Evie decided she was too tired to argue and nibbled at the corner of the bread as he stalked away.

He came back with two cups of coffee and straddled the chair opposite hers. "So you're going home. I think you're making the right decision—"

A chunk of crust took an unexpected detour down the wrong pipe. "Not my home," she managed to choke. "Dad's *home*."

Sam stared at her. "You're still planning to stay after what happened today? Knowing Seth is still interested in whatever he thinks you have? Knowing you might be in trouble?"

When he put it that way…

"Yes." She cloaked the word in bravery, leaning on the passage of scripture she'd tucked in her heart.

You will keep in perfect peace him whose mind is steadfast, because he trusts in you….

Sam's chair scraped against the floor as he pushed it away and rose to his feet. "Brainy, beautiful…and bullheaded."

Chapter Twelve

Evie decided two out of three wasn't so bad.

Still, Sam barely said two words to her on the way home. But he insisted on checking to make sure Beach Glass was still locked up tight and no one had broken into the house.

If his intent was to make her nervous, he was doing a stellar job.

He circled the kitchen and paused next to the telephone. "Looks like you have a message."

"Maybe it's Dad." Evie punched the button and listened impatiently while the prerecorded message went through the standard pleasantries.

"Ah...Miss McBride?" She gulped when she heard Seth Lansky's familiar voice. And it didn't sound half as friendly as it had when he'd asked her to help him with the passwords! "I want to talk and I think you know why. I'll be in touch. Soon."

The worst part was, Evie *didn't* know why.

"Change your mind?" Sam growled.

Evie shook her head. Because she couldn't form a coherent sentence even if she tried.

"I'll be right back." He gave her a look that clearly questioned her sanity and finished his rounds. After he rattled the sliding glass doors, Evie stepped in his path.

"If you wait a few minutes, I'll give you your clothes back. Or I can give them to you tomorrow when I meet with Faith."

"Tomorrow's Saturday. Faith and I are going out on the boat for the weekend."

"Overnight?" Evie's voice raised a notch.

"I believe the weekend would include an overnight, yes."

Evie's back teeth clamped together. She knew he was being difficult because she refused to take his advice and leave.

"I'm sure Faith will enjoy it," she said sweetly. "She has fifty math problems to finish by Monday and I'd like her to read the next short story in her literature book."

"I'll see she gets it done." Sam pivoted away from her and headed toward the door.

"Sam! Wait a second. I forgot something." Evie disappeared into her father's office and returned with a small, leather-bound book. "Here."

Sam stared down at the book. "What's that?"

"A Bible. I told Faith I'd lend her one. Remember?" When he made no move to take it, Evie pressed it gently into his hands.

Sam's thumb grazed the words embossed in gold on the cover. "I suppose it can't hurt."

Evie's heart softened when she saw the shadows skim through his eyes. "Faith was fascinated by the story of the loaves and fishes. Tell her to look up Matthew, the first book of the New Testament, and go to the fifteenth chapter." *God, what should I say to him? He doesn't realize he's holding the power to change his life.* "I read one of the Psalms every morning."

"Why?"

Was he baiting her? Evie decided it didn't matter. She wouldn't pass up an opportunity to share the truth. "The Psalmist, a man named David, didn't always understand God's ways but he wanted to know Him. And he wasn't afraid to ask Him tough questions along the way."

"Did God answer his questions?" Sam's voice carried an undercurrent of cynicism now.

"Not always," Evie said honestly. "But we don't find peace by having all our questions answered. We find it in God. He loves us and we can trust Him to bring something good out of everything that happens in our lives."

Pain darkened Sam's eyes. "Tell that to my brother."

* * *

"Faith? Are you ready to go yet?" Sam rapped his knuckles lightly against the fluorescent yellow Enter At Your Own Risk poster taped to the door.

He'd let Faith sleep away half the morning and then she'd holed up in her cabin again after breakfast. He hadn't minded being on deck alone to greet the sunrise. For the second restless night in a row, he'd watched the stars fade away one by one. Ordinarily he slept like the dead when they anchored the boat in one of the shallow bays for the night, lulled by the fresh air and the rocking motion of the waves. But not this time.

"You can come in if you want."

Sam gripped his chest with one hand and pretended to stagger. "Really? To the inner sanctum?"

There was a noisy exhale on the other side of the door. "That's what I said."

He chuckled and accepted the invitation before Faith changed her mind. "I'm surprised you aren't topside barking orders."

Reluctant as Faith had been to come to Cooper's Landing, she'd turned into a first-class first mate. She loved being on the water as much as he did. Not that Lake Superior provided an instant cure for the roller coaster of adolescence, but Faith seemed to be smiling a little more. And she'd even forgiven him for interrupting her unauthorized phone call to the care facility the day before.

Maybe it's Evie you should thank.

Sam shook the thought away even though he knew another one would replace it soon enough. That was the trouble. He couldn't *stop* thinking about Evie. The way she'd held it together and taken care of Faith when Seth had followed them into the woods. Her stubborn insistence on staying even though worry clouded her eyes.

He was starting to realize he'd underestimated her. Maybe she didn't laugh in the face of danger but she wasn't afraid to stare it down, either. And her faith was a wild card he had no clue how to deal with…

There you go again.

Sam yanked his wayward thoughts back in line and focused his attention on his niece, who lay on her back on the bunk bed, Evie's Bible propped against her knees.

"I wanted to finish reading something."

"Shouldn't you be doing homework?" As far as hints went, not so subtle, but the sight of Faith reading her Bible unsettled him. He still wasn't sure how Dan and Rachel would feel about it. He didn't know how *he* felt about it.

"I finished my math." Faith looked up at him. "Did you know Jesus healed people?"

"Uh-huh." Vague, but the best he could do on short notice.

"It says in here He healed all kinds of people. People who were blind and deaf." She paused for a second and sucked in her lower lip. "Even people who couldn't…walk."

It didn't take a biblical scholar to know where Faith was going with that. And Sam felt totally, completely out of his element.

He'd been there when Faith had let go of Dan's fingers and took her first wobbly steps. He'd taught her how to ice skate, slam dunk and do a mean imitation of a Tarzan yell. Although Rachel had never quite forgiven him for the last one.

Faith waited expectantly and Sam's throat closed. It was like seeing Dan all over again. Looking to him for answers. For comfort. For whatever.

You're wrong, Dad, Sam thought. You said all I had to do was look inside myself and I'd find everything I need to tackle whatever life throws at me. Well, I'm coming up empty here. I've got nothing. Nothing for Dan. Nothing for Faith. Nothing for *me*.

"Evie told me the Bible is true." Faith tested the silence when he didn't respond right away.

"A lot of people believe that." People who, according to Jacob, didn't have the strength and know-how to solve their own problems.

"Do you?"

Sam gave up and sat down at the foot of the bed. "I've never thought about it much." At least not until Dan was hurt. Ever since then he'd been bombarded by the same relentless questions. What happened when a man's life changed in an instant and he reached the end of his own strength? What took over?

"Evie told me I should pray for Dad. If I do…"

Sam winced, bracing himself.

"Do you think he'll laugh again?"

The question sucker punched him. He'd expected Faith to say she wanted her dad to walk again. But she hadn't. She missed hearing him laugh. Easygoing and fun-loving, Dan loved practical jokes. No one was exempt as a target, whether it was the guys who worked his shift at the police department or his immediate family. Sam had lost track of how many times his brother had set him up over the years.

Regret burned through Sam, leaving a bitter taste in his mouth. The last time he'd heard Dan laugh was the day his brother was injured, when he'd called to invite Sam over for the weekend to celebrate Faith's birthday. The phone call he'd received three hours later had been from a near-hysterical Rachel, telling him Dan had been shot while responding to a call for a domestic disturbance. He and his partner were walking toward the house when a guy, strung out on drugs, aimed a shotgun out the second-story window and opened fire. Diving for cover, Dan had been hit an inch below his Kevlar vest.

Sam tried to think of a way to encourage his niece without getting her hopes up too high. "Your dad is trying to find his way, Faith. And if you want to pray for him, go ahead."

Maybe God wouldn't listen to the prayers of a man like him, who'd always relied on himself, but Sam hoped He wouldn't turn a deaf ear to those of a young girl who wanted to hear her dad laugh again.

Faith turned her head away and Sam knew she didn't want him to see the tear sliding down her face. Too late. Now he'd do anything to see *her* smile.

Since they'd arrived in Cooper's Landing, he'd handled Faith's moods by retreating and giving her space because that's how *he* coped with pain. But Evie had shot that theory all to bits the day she'd brought over that rusty basketball hoop.

Surround Faith with the things she loves and everything else will fall into place.

He'd try it Evie's way.

"Why don't we stop by Sophie's when we get to shore and borrow Rocky for the rest of the day?"

"Really? Can we go now?" Faith sat up and hugged her knees.

"Sure." And maybe they'd stop by Evie's afterward. To drop off Faith's homework.

Sciurus carolinensis.

Evie groaned and yanked a pillow over her head to muffle the chatter of her alarm clock. Which happened to be the gray squirrel perched in the tree outside her window. At six o'clock on Sunday morning.

Fifteen minutes later, she gave up and tossed the covers aside. She peered at the squirrel through the screen. Now he sat on the empty feeder, his tail twitching with indignation. "Fine. You win. I'll replenish your corn supply."

Evie staggered to the kitchen in her pajamas, made a pot of coffee and poured herself a cup. Sunlight pooled on the hardwood floor, and in the distance the glittering surface of the lake looked as if it had been sprinkled with gold dust.

The heavens declare the glory of God; the skies proclaim the work of His hands.

The opening verse of Psalm 19 scrolled through her mind as she closed her eyes and said good morning to the Lord.

It's beautiful, God. You do all things well.

For a brief moment, she wished she could be out on the water. To feel the breeze brush against her skin. Have a front-row view of the towering sandstone bluffs. Watch the seagulls circling overhead in a graceful synchronized choreography. Experience…a severe case of nausea.

Evie decided she didn't have to be standing on the deck of a boat to enjoy God's creation. She could just be on a…deck. To prove her point, she took her Bible outside. Bypassing her dad's hammock, which, she noted critically, probably wasn't good for his back, she chose a cushioned cedar chair and flopped into it.

Curious black-capped chickadees landed on the

railing to take a look at her, and Evie shared her bran muffin with them before closing her eyes and spending time in prayer. Armed with scripture she'd memorized over the years, she aimed a verse at every worry that crowded into her thoughts. She prayed for Patrick and Jacob. Sophie. Faith. Faith's parents. And for Sam.

Father, I think that Sam wants to talk to You but he doesn't know how. Reveal Yourself to him. Show him that he can find hope in You.

Thank You for watching out for me and Faith yesterday. I know You want Your people to be courageous and I fall so short of that. I'm tempted to go home but if You want me to be here for Faith, I'll stay and I'll trust You.

Evie kept her eyes closed for a few minutes, softly humming the tune to one of her favorite praise choruses. Within moments, a verse drifted soft as a breeze into her thoughts.

Trust in the Lord with all your heart and lean not on your own understanding. In all your ways acknowledge Him, and He will make your paths straight.

Thank you for the reminder, Lord.

That's what she wanted Sam to understand. If he turned to God even when life didn't make sense, God wouldn't let him down.

She glanced at her watch, calculated how much time she'd need to get ready for church and decided she had time to take a short detour.

Chapter Thirteen

"I'm so glad you called." Sophie smiled as Evie opened the passenger side of the door and waited for her to slide in. "I was just thinking how lonely church would be this morning without your father to keep me company."

Tyson could go with you.

Evie bit the inside of her lip to prevent her from saying it out loud. When she'd stopped by to pick up Sophie, Tyson had been sound asleep on the couch.

"I didn't want to go alone, either," she said instead.

"I made chicken salad and a loaf of banana bread last night," Sophie said. "Can you stay for lunch?"

"I'd love to." The older woman's offer of friendship wrapped around her like a warm blanket. Caitlin and Meghan would love Sophie if they had a chance to meet her. And Evie had a feeling they would.

She looked forward to spending a few more hours

with Sophie but hoped Tyson wouldn't be at the house when they returned. Evie made a habit not to judge people by the way they looked, but the unease she felt around Sophie's son wasn't due to his hygienically challenged outward appearance. Something in Tyson's cool, flat stare made her question what was going on on the *inside.*

Evie started her car and maneuvered it out of the church parking lot. "I came here for worship services last summer when I stayed a few weeks with Dad, but I don't remember seeing you."

"That's because I didn't know the Lord last summer," Sophie said matter-of-factly.

Evie blinked. "I... The way you talked about God and the way you prayed... I assumed you'd been a believer for years."

Sophie chuckled. "I'm afraid it's been just the opposite! You can give your father the credit for introducing us. When everyone else brought bestselling novels to read to the patients at the hospital, Patrick brought his Bible." Her eyes twinkled. "I have to admit there were a few times I wanted to throw it at him, but I didn't have the strength! He had a captive audience and he knew it. I couldn't get rid of him, so I started to listen to what he was saying.

"One afternoon he read a story about a woman who'd been sick for years. She risked everything to get close enough to Jesus to touch his robe. She wanted a new life. I could relate to her. The one thing

I'd always wished for was the chance to live my life over again. Growing up, my family wasn't the kind you read about in storybooks. I met Tyson's father and hoped things would be different, but he walked out on us when Tyson was ten years old. I'd been wallowing in the past, wishing things had been different. The day Patrick read that passage I realized I wanted God to heal me, too. Not physically, but from the pain I'd lived with on the *inside*." Sophie's face took on a radiant glow. "Your father prayed with me when I gave my life to Jesus."

Tears stung Evie's eyes. Patrick had always had a gift for pointing people to the truth. She wasn't surprised he'd known exactly what story would touch Sophie's heart. "I'm glad Dad was there for you."

"So am I. Me and the Lord, we have a lot of catching up to do. I wasted so many years trying to muddle through life on my own." A shadow momentarily dimmed the light in Sophie's eyes. "Like Jacob."

"Jacob *Cutter?*" Evie asked cautiously.

"I've been on my knees for that man so often, I'm going to have to sew patches over the worn spots on my slacks," Sophie said. "Just about the time Patrick and I sensed him softening, his son was badly injured and he closed up again. When he came back from Chicago last month, he was so bitter. He made both of us promise we wouldn't talk about God." Sophie's smile returned. "But we never promised we wouldn't talk to God about *him*."

Evie laughed with her even as her heart ached for the Cutters. When Laura died, Patrick's unwavering faith had been a light that guided Evie through the dark valleys of grief. From the pain in Sam's eyes, it was clear he was stumbling through the shadows, looking for something to hold on to.

"Look at that." Sophie clucked her tongue as Evie turned the car into the driveway. "Tyson is almost thirty years old and he still forgets to shut the door when he leaves. It's a good thing I locked Sadie and the puppies up in the laundry room or they'd be in the next county by now."

Evie followed Sophie inside and heard Sadie whining behind a door off the kitchen. The puppies joined her in a chorus of frantic yips.

"Tyson?" Sophie called above the commotion. "Are you here? We have company for lunch."

The hair on the back of Evie's neck tingled suddenly. Something wasn't right. Other than the sound of Sadie's obvious distress, an eerie silence filled the house. And that open door…

"Sophie, wait."

"I'll be right back." Sophie disappeared into the den and suddenly a sharp cry pierced the air.

"What is it? What's wrong?" Evie bolted into the room and her vision blurred as she took in the scene in front of her.

The room had been ripped apart. Furniture overturned. Shards of what had once been the porcelain figures in Sophie's curio cabinet littered the floor like confetti. The rolltop desk had been hacked to pieces.

Evie couldn't swallow. Had to consciously remind herself to breathe. "Sophie—"

Sophie knelt in the middle of the destruction, sifting through the papers scattered on the floor. "They're gone, Evie. The letters. The newspaper articles. Everything."

"Look! Evie's here." Faith squealed in delight at the sight of the familiar vehicle parked in Sophie's driveway.

Sam barely had the car in Park when she unbuckled her seat belt and launched herself out the door.

Sam followed at a more leisurely pace, the relief of knowing Evie was safe and sound soaking into his subconscious. He hadn't wanted to admit his concern for her had been part of the reason he'd given up a beautiful day on the open water and come back to shore early.

After her near miss with Seth on Friday and the cryptic phone message he'd left, Sam thought for sure she would agree to leave. Not knowing what Seth wanted or how much of a threat he posed had to make Evie feel vulnerable. She'd said herself that she didn't like surprises and the structured way she lived her life proved it.

So why couldn't he convince her to leave?

God brought me to Cooper's Landing.

Sam remembered the reason Evie had given and

he rolled his eyes toward the sky. Billions of people inhabited the world. Sam had serious doubts that God had noticed one twelve-year-old girl who was failing her classes and that He had sent someone to help her. Even if he couldn't dismiss the fact that Evie, with her unwavering faith and loving concern, had somehow unlocked the key to Faith's heart.

Like she was trying to do to his.

When Faith wasn't paying attention, he'd snuck a look at the Psalms, the book Evie said she read from every day. The brutal honesty of the writer surprised him but what shocked him even more was that God hadn't taken the guy out for hammering Him with questions.

It eased the knot in his chest. He had a lot of questions, too, but he still wasn't sure how to ask them.

Sam reached out to grab the handle on the front door just as Faith blasted through it, almost toppling him back down the steps.

"Faith, for crying out loud—" The panic in her eyes squeezed the air out of his lungs.

"Sophie," Faith gasped.

Sam didn't wait for a longer explanation. He pushed open the door and met Evie on the other side.

"What happened? Is Sophie all right?"

"She's fine. But someone broke into the house." Evie's voice wobbled and Sam took her hand. Ice-cold. Automatically, he rubbed his thumb against her palm to stimulate the circulation.

"Where is she?"

"In here." Evie led him into the den and Sam exhaled slowly as he took a quick inventory of the damage. Whoever had broken in had had something specific in mind. And, judging from the amount of senseless vandalism, an ax to grind.

Sophie occupied the same chair she'd sat in the night she'd told them about Patrick and Jacob's search for the *Noble*. A search that had gotten out of control. Maybe it had started out innocently enough, like a trickle of water during a spring thaw, but now it had picked up both strength and speed. And was running roughshod over everything in its path.

"Have you called the police yet?" Sam recognized the shell-shocked look in Sophie's eyes and directed the question at Evie instead. She stood just inside the room, one arm looped around Faith, who'd wilted against her with Rocky cradled tightly in her arms.

"Not yet. We just got here."

"Evie and I went to church," Sophie added. "I don't know where Tyson is. When we walked in, we found this. Whoever broke in took everything Patrick and I collected about the *Noble*. It was all locked in a desk drawer. I don't know yet if anything else is missing."

"I'll be right back," Evie murmured. "I'm going to get Sophie a glass of water."

With a wide-eyed, fearful look at Sophie, Faith followed Evie out the door. After they'd gone, Sam dropped into the chair opposite Sophie and leaned toward her. "Was there any sign of forced entry?"

"No. But we never lock the door. There's been no need."

"And you said Tyson was here when you left?"

Sophie nodded. "He came home quite late. He must have been too tired to go upstairs because he was asleep on the couch when I came down this morning. I didn't want to disturb him."

Too tired or too drunk? Sam decided not to ask. The break-in was enough for Sophie to handle at the moment.

"I'll call the police and ask them to send over a deputy. They'll take photographs, so we can't clean up the mess yet. Have you checked the rest of the house?"

"No." Sophie closed her eyes. "I can replace the newspaper articles but not Dorothea's letters and my great-grandmother's journal. I can't believe someone would do this."

Sam could.

"The *Noble* would be quite a feather in a treasure hunter's cap," he said quietly. "Not only because it's a new find but because there might be something valuable on board." And Sam was more convinced than ever that whoever wanted to find the *Noble* wasn't going to bother obeying the salvage laws.

"I know Patrick and Jacob didn't say a word to anyone about the treasure. And according to Jacob, he and Bruce Mullins were like brothers when they served together in the Marines. You know your father doesn't confide in people easily—he wouldn't be meeting with Bruce about the ship if he wasn't sure he could trust him."

Evie returned and Sophie accepted the glass of water she gently pressed into her hand. "Do you think that man, Seth Lansky, did this?"

Before Sam had a chance to comment, a strangled sound came from the doorway.

"Mom?" Tyson hurried into the room, fear etched in his face as he dropped to his knees in front of his mother and took her hands. "Are you all right?"

"I've had better mornings, honey," Sophie said, a faint glimmer of humor returning to her eyes.

"What happened?" Tyson's gaze swept the den and his lips went slack as he saw the extent of the damage.

Sam speared Tyson with a look. Sophie might want to downplay the seriousness of the situation for her son but that didn't mean Sam had to make it all touchy-feely for him. "How long were you gone?"

He hadn't meant for it to sound like an accusation, but Tyson scowled, immediately on the defensive.

"Not more than half an hour. I went into Cooper's Landing to get a newspaper to check the classifieds for jobs."

Which meant someone had been hanging around, watching and waiting for an opportunity to get inside the house. Sam's fists clenched at his sides. Lansky must have decided breaking and entering was a quicker way to get what he wanted than lying his way in, like he'd tried to do with Evie.

"Tyson, after I call the police, why don't we check out the upstairs to make sure nothing else is missing," Sam suggested. "Your mom will need a list when she makes a claim to the insurance company."

Resentment simmered in Tyson's eyes but he pushed to his feet. "What did they take, Mom? The computer? The DVD player?"

Yeah, because life just wouldn't be the same without that stuff, Sam thought in disgust. The molecule of respect that had formed when he'd witnessed Tyson's initial concern for his mother evaporated like a drop of water on a hot skillet.

"I'm not sure yet," Sophie said vaguely. "But Sam's right. You go with him and see if anything is missing upstairs."

Tyson's gaze lingered on the demolished rolltop desk. "Did you have anything valuable in there?"

Sophie smiled sadly. "Valuable, no. Irreplaceable, yes."

Sam saw the confusion that skimmed across Tyson's face. Apparently the guy didn't realize there was a difference.

By the time the deputies from the sheriff's department left, Evie felt as if she'd been put through the spin cycle of a washing machine. One deputy snapped photographs of the den while another took statements from her and Sophie.

Sophie listed the missing items but didn't offer any reason as to why she thought they'd been taken. Some old coins locked in the desk were stolen, too, and Sophie didn't correct the deputy's assumption they must have been what the perpetrator had wanted.

Something about Sophie's reticence caused Evie to resist the temptation to tell the deputy about Seth Lansky. When it came right down to it, what did she know about him? He hadn't broken in and stolen her dad's computer. He hadn't even threatened her that day in the woods or on the message he'd left on the answering machine. Suspicions were the only evidence they had.

Sam and Tyson escorted the deputies to the squad car, and Evie shooed Faith and the puppies outside so she could tackle the mess in the den. She found a broom and began to sweep up shattered glass while Sophie collected the pieces of desk that littered the floor.

They worked in silence until Evie happened to glance at Sophie and saw tears tracking her cheeks.

"Sophie?" Evie scrambled over to her and put her arm around the woman's shoulders, mentally chiding herself for not banning Sophie to the living room with a cup of hot tea.

"Let me make you a cup of tea and something to eat." Evie guided her into the kitchen and into one of the wooden chairs at the table. She rummaged through the refrigerator until she found a block of aged cheddar cheese and some crisp apples and set to work cutting them up.

"As soon as we get in touch with your father, I'm going to insist he and Jacob come back." Sophie's voice barely broke above a whisper. "And I'm going to tell them to give up the search. Family is more valuable than any silly treasure that might be on board the *Noble*. What if Tyson had been home during the break-in? He could have been hurt. It's not worth the risk."

Ordinarily, Evie would have agreed. Maybe she *should* have agreed. But anger welled up inside her at the thought of people who didn't think twice about terrorizing a woman and destroying her property.

"I don't think Dad would want to give up," she heard herself saying. "And I don't think we should, either."

Chapter Fourteen

Had Sam really thought that Evie McBride, with her love of schedules and I-don't-like-surprises personality, was *predictable?*

Because she wasn't. In fact, she was turning out to be predictably *unpredictable.*

"What are you planning?" He could practically *see* the wheels turning in those big blue eyes.

"I'm going to call Caitlin and ask her if she remembers the name of the last goldfish Meghan forgot to feed, and then I'm going to access Dad's computer files and make new copies of the documents for Sophie so Dad will have them when he gets back."

It was worse than he'd thought.

"Are you out of your mind?" Sam whispered in her ear, matching his steps to Evie's as they walked to her car.

Evie adjusted the gigantic purse—probably to

balance the amount of strain on her shoulder—and looked him right in the eye. "No."

"I'm sorry. Did you think that was a question? I meant it as a statement."

"Dad wouldn't give up."

"He might not give up, but that doesn't mean he wouldn't want *you* to," Sam pointed out, feeling it necessary to do so. "He and my dad have no idea Sophie's place was broken into. Tyson is so freaked out he actually insisted Sophie stay with her minister and his wife for a few days."

"That's good. It shows he cares about her, although I don't think he's exactly bodyguard material."

Did she think he was? Because Sam was taking on the job whether he wanted to or not. He'd lost enough sleep over the weekend worrying about her safety. If he couldn't convince her to leave, there had to be some way he could keep a closer eye on her.

"I'll be over tomorrow afternoon to meet with Faith."

Faith heard her name and darted over, Rocky at her heels. "Can I keep your Bible a few more days, Evie?"

"Keep it as long as you like. It's an extra." Evie reeled Faith in for a hug, and Faith didn't squirm, kick or try to set Evie on fire with a glare.

Sam sighed.

Go figure.

Evie paced the floor for fifteen minutes, trying to decide which sister to call first. Caitlin had a memory like a steel trap and would no doubt be able to rattle off the names of all the goldfish the McBride sisters had nurtured throughout their childhood. But she'd also insist on knowing *why* Evie wanted her to remember them.

Meghan, on the other hand, wouldn't think to ask why, but she did have a tendency to be forgetful. Sticky notes wallpapered her apartment. And if Meghan didn't remember a cache of miniature chocolate bars hidden in her pillowcase—until after she put the pillowcase in the washing machine— Evie wasn't too sure she'd remember the name of the fourth goldfish that had taken up residence in the McBride household.

Evie took a deep breath and dialed Caitlin's cell. And got her voice mail.

"Hi, this is Caitlin McBride. I can't take your call right now but if this is Meghan, don't forget to mail out your car insurance. It's due this month. And if this is Evie, check your e-mail once in a while, would you? If you're a client, I'll get back to you as soon as possible. And have a nice day."

Check your e-mail.

Evie groaned. She hadn't booted up her laptop since she'd arrived. Patrick didn't have Internet service, although he'd mentioned the café in Cooper's Landing now boasted a wireless connection.

With only the songbirds at the feeder for company, Evie suddenly felt isolated and alone. And despite her confident words to Sam, she still felt a bit shaken from the break-in at Sophie's.

She'd called the lodge to find out if there'd been any word from Patrick and Jacob, but the proprietor had politely suggested she call back in a few days. Out of touch with her dad, Evie had a sudden longing to reconnect with her sisters. She decided it wouldn't hurt to drive into Cooper's Landing and get a cup of coffee while she caught up on her messages. At least that way, when she talked to Caitlin she could honestly tell her that she'd read them!

Evie didn't expect to see Sam and Faith until the next day, but when she got out of the car and paused to admire the sparkling sapphire water, there was no mistaking the tall, lean frame walking the shoreline. Or the puppy bouncing like a furry pogo stick at his feet.

Evie scanned the beach and relaxed when she spotted Faith, who'd staked a claim just out of reach of the waves to build a sand castle.

To Evie's astonishment, Sam flopped down next to Faith and began to scoop handfuls of wet sand to assist her in the project. Even from the distance separating them, she could see him laughing at something Faith said. And then he picked up a plastic shovel and used it to catapult water at her. Faith retaliated by soaking him with the contents of the moat she'd dug around the castle.

He'll be a great dad.

Even as the errant thought took root and bloomed, Evie felt her cheeks glow underneath the thin layer of tinted sunscreen she'd applied before she left the house.

And the practical side of her nature immediately voiced its disapproval.

Sure. He'll be one of those dads who take the training wheels off too soon. Or let the kids play tackle football in the backyard without the proper padding.

And if his wife dared to express her concerns, she'd be labeled the family stick-in-the-mud. No fun. No sense of adventure.

No, thank you.

Still, she had to resist the sudden, overwhelming urge to forget about her e-mail and run down to the beach to join them.

She walked into the café and realized the rest of the world had decided to spend a beautiful Sunday afternoon *outside*. Every table was empty.

A teenage waitress wandered out of the kitchen. "You can sit anywhere you want to."

Mmm. A table with an unobstructed view of Cooper's Landing's quaint Main Street or a table with an unobstructed view of Sam?

She chose the table overlooking Main Street. Not as distracting. She put in an order for pie and coffee and opened her laptop.

The first three e-mails were from Caitlin. All of them began with a complaint about the lack of cell-phone towers in the "wilderness" and demanded to know why Evie was ignoring her. Evie suppressed a smile. Caitlin wasn't used to being ignored.

Meghan had written, too, accidentally sending her the same message twice, inquiring about their dad and expressing envy over Evie's "relaxing" summer vacation.

Evie rolled her eyes. She hadn't gotten past the dedication page on the first novel she'd intended to read, and the tomato plants she'd brought along were still waiting to be transplanted into their new containers on the deck.

Oh, it's relaxing all right, Meggie.

She erased some spam, skimmed through some general e-mails from the school administrator and came to one that said "Matthew 620" in the subject line. The sender's address wasn't familiar, and the last thing Evie wanted to do was set a virus loose in her hard drive.

Her finger hovered over the delete button. Some of her students had asked for her e-mail address so they could keep in contact over the summer, and she didn't want to inadvertently ignore one of them.

"Here goes." Evie clicked on the message and instantly a lithograph-type photo of an old map downloaded onto the screen. Along with a message from her father.

"But store up for yourselves treasures in heaven, where moth and rust do not destroy, and where thieves do not break in and steal. For where your treasure is, there your heart also will be." Matthew 6: 20, 21

Evie, please share this verse with Sophie. It's one of my favorites. See you soon.

Love, Dad

"Well, Patty McBride, aren't you just full of surprises?" Evie muttered, eyeing the verse superimposed over a sepia-toned map. "I didn't think you knew how to send an e-mail message let alone a background...."

Her heart slipped into the toes of her sensible shoes as she realized what she was looking at.

Seth Lansky had made a critical mistake. Patrick hadn't stored the latest information about the *Noble* on his computer.

He'd sent it to hers.

"Sam?"

It had to be a hallucination. One minute Sam was staring at the water, thinking it was an exact match to Evie's eyes, and the next thing he knew, he heard her voice.

"Hi, Evie!" Faith jumped to her feet, kicking a spray of golden, sun-warmed sand against his leg. "What are you doing here?"

For a split second, Sam thought Evie had changed her mind and accepted Faith's invitation to spend the afternoon with them on the beach. Until he saw her expression. A warning bell clanged in his head.

"Look at the castle we made."

"It's great." Evie's smile seemed forced as she bent down to examine it.

Sam frowned. More warning bells. Tension coiled in his gut. Now what? Something to do with Sophie? Or their fathers?

"I put the flowers on it and Sam put the rocks along the top. To protect it from invaders." Faith rolled her eyes.

"Hey, you thought it was a good idea at the time." Sam gave Faith's ponytail a playful tug.

She dodged away from him. "I'll be right back. I'm going to find some sticks and leaves to make flags. Can you stay for a little while, Evie?"

"A few minutes."

"Good." Faith grinned. "I can give you a tour of the *Natalie*."

If anything, Evie's skin paled even more and she managed a jerky nod.

Sam waited until Faith was out of earshot. "Okay, what's up? I know you didn't come down here to build sand castles with Faith." He wished she would have. She'd stepped out of her comfort zone to play basketball, but the nervous little glances she directed toward the water, as if she were imagining a rogue wave rising out of nowhere and pulling her under, shot that hope all to pieces.

"Dad sent me an e-mail dated the day before I got here. The day he called Sophie and told her he had good news." She paused.

Okay, he'd bite. "What did it say?"

"I'd rather show you. I have my laptop in my purse. Can you take a few minutes and go to the café with me? I'll treat Faith to an ice-cream cone."

Was he imagining the faint glimmer of excitement in her eyes? "I doubt the owner of the café would believe Rocky is a service dog."

She gnawed on her lower lip. "Oh. I didn't think about him—"

"Do you want to see the boat now?" Faith returned, the puppy at her heels.

"Evie suggested ice cream." Sam stepped in, figuring Evie had already reached her quota of traumatic experiences for the day. "Why don't you keep working on the castle and we'll bring some back from the café?"

"That's all right." Evie smiled bravely. "I can see the boat first."

She continued to surprise him. He'd tried to let her off the hook, but once again she'd stepped out of her comfort zone for Faith. His respect for Evie went up another notch. Who was he kidding? Another ten notches. And suddenly Sam realized the needle gauging his emotions had somehow snuck past "like" and was hovering perilously close to…something else.

Sam's jaw locked. Attraction, maybe. That wasn't

as scary. He wasn't blind. No one could blame a guy for getting caught in the depths of a pair of wide, sapphire-blue eyes. Or for knowing exactly how many cinnamon freckles dotted her nose. *Twelve.* But he didn't want to care about Evie McBride. Not that way.

Dan's injury had cut him loose from his moorings, setting him adrift in a sea of questions and doubt. The Cutter pride was the only thing keeping him from going under and who knew how long *that* was going to keep him afloat? Every time he remembered Dan saying that he wished he'd died on the way to the E.R., Sam felt his grip slipping a little more. The last thing he wanted to do was to pull someone else down with him.

Like Evie.

No, *not* just Evie. Not anybody.

"Okay, Faith, go ahead and lead the way." Evie marched stoically toward the dock as if she were going to have to walk the plank when she boarded the *Natalie.* Her purse bumped against her hip like unsecured cargo. Knowing how much stuff she had in that thing, she'd probably end up with bruises that wouldn't fade for a month.

"You don't have to do this, you know." Sam eased the bag off her shoulder and looped it over his arm, ignoring her look of surprise. He shrugged. "At least it's khaki and not pink with polka dots."

Her smile made a serious dent in the armor around his heart. "According to Caitlin, pink clashes with *this.*" She sifted strands of silky, red-gold hair through her fingers. "My wardrobe consists of greens and browns and golds. And I accent with pumpkin."

"You lost me." Because the way the sunlight played on her hair had his full attention at the moment. He scrambled to catch up. "Who is Caitlin?"

"My older sister. The *oldest* sister. And proof that everything you hear about first-born overachievers is true." Evie's eyes sparkled with obvious affection. "She works as an image consultant in Minneapolis and she has a lot of important clients. I surrendered my closet a long time ago, but so far Meghan, that's my other sister, refuses to be conquered."

"What does Meghan do?"

"She's a freelance photographer. She's in New England right now, working on a series of calendar photos for a private company. She and Cait are both pretty busy."

He detected a thread of wistfulness in her voice. "Which leaves Evie. A teacher with summers off. That must be nice."

"It is." She didn't sound very convincing. "I miss my students, but it gives me a chance to spend time with Dad. He gets lonely."

He *gets lonely,* Sam thought with a sudden flash of insight, *or* you *get lonely?*

He'd assumed from comments Jacob had made that Evie acted like a mother hen when it came to her father, but now he wondered if there wasn't another reason for it.

"Do you travel much when you aren't teaching?" *Way to keep your distance, Cutter. Ask her about her life.*

"No." Evie slowed her pace as they neared the dock. "I read. Garden. That sort of thing. I put in so many hours at school that I'd rather stay home when I have the chance." She paused and dug a half circle in the sand with the toe of her shoe. "What do you do in your free time? Besides boating?"

She was stalling. Sam suppressed a smile. "I do some rock climbing. Sailing. Fly fishing." And he'd done every one of those things with Dan. Regret rocketed through him again. He'd lost sleep wondering how Dan would cope if he couldn't enjoy his favorite activities, but until this moment, Sam hadn't looked at it from his own perspective. Would *he* still enjoy them?

"Sam? Are you all right?"

When he glanced down at Evie, he wondered why she thought she'd needed to mix up a homemade bomb that day in the woods. The incredible blue eyes focused on him created enough of a distraction. She was five yards away from a dock that looked as if it had been built out of toothpicks, but the concern in her eyes was for *him.*

"I'm great." He lied through his teeth as he sealed up his emotions in a space marked by a sign similar to the one on Faith's door. Do Not Disturb.

Faith waved to them from the deck of the *Natalie.* "Come on, you slowpokes."

Sam hopped up on the dock and took three steps before he realized Evie wasn't following him. She stared at the boat, her complexion a bit green. She already looked seasick.

"She's tied up, Evie."

"*She's* still…bobbing."

Sam chuckled. "Boats tend to do that. Especially on the water." He retraced his steps, caught her hand and gave a gentle tug. She responded by digging her sensible shoes into the weathered wood and tugging back.

"I'm a coward," she murmured. "Ask my sisters. I don't like being on the water."

"In that case, you're good to go. You'll be on the boat, not the water." Still holding her hand, Sam urged her closer to the *Natalie*. He had to do some-thing drastic to wipe the panicked look off her face. He remembered Evie's tendency to get defensive about her purse, so he let it go and it hit the deck with a dull thud. "We already have an anchor, but thanks."

"Very funny." Evie snatched it up but he noticed with relief that some of her color had returned.

Sam leaped across the narrow space separating the boat from the dock and stretched out his hand. "Ready?"

"Come on, Evie. You'll love it." Faith joined in the cheering section.

Evie cast another longing look at the beach.

"Come on, Evie. Trust me. I'm an expert at catch

and release." Sam winked at her and Evie's burst of laughter went straight to his heart.

"That I can believe."

Chapter Fifteen

Evie focused on Sam's smoke-gray eyes instead of the enormous expanse of blue in the background. And jumped. True to his word, he steadied her and then promptly let her go. For a split second, disappointment outweighed her fear of the water.

"Faith, why don't you bring up a pitcher of lemonade. All that castle building works up a thirst."

"Sure." Faith disappeared down the short flight of steps that led below deck, and Sam motioned to Evie. "Step into my office and tell me about the message."

Evie perched in one of the captain's chairs, not sure where to begin. "Dad asked me to share a verse from Matthew with Sophie. That was strange enough, because he could have done that himself. But the background the verse is printed on is a…map."

"A map," Sam repeated.

Evie didn't take offense at Sam's skeptical look.

It *did* sound a little far-fetched. She had her own doubts until she'd studied it more closely. "On the map, there's a ship just off the north end of a small island. It would make sense that the *Noble* would sail for the shelter of a bay if it got into trouble."

"You don't know if the ship depicted on the map is the *Noble.* Patrick could have pasted in that image from an old book or a pamphlet from a tourist center. It might not mean anything."

"That's why I *know* it means something. The map isn't a copy—he drew it himself." And the lines he'd drawn overlapped at the same point. On the tiny sketch of a ship.

"Even if Patrick has a general idea where the ship went down, don't you think if it sank that close to one of the islands, someone would have discovered it by now? Professional and recreational divers have combed this area for years." Sam scraped a hand through his hair in frustration. "And if by chance it is there and no one's found it, it means we won't, either. It's too deep or a reef smashed it to pieces and there's nothing left to find."

"Maybe. But that must be why our dads wanted to meet with Bruce Mullins. To find out if it was worth taking a look. When Sophie and I were on our way to church this morning, she mentioned Dad had found some old diary entries from a sawyer who had worked at one of the logging camps. He didn't have a chance to show them to her, but maybe

Dad based the map on something he'd discovered written in them."

"You told Sophie about the map?"

Evie frowned at the sudden undercurrent of tension she heard in his voice. "I called her from the café. I thought she'd want to know that whoever stole the records didn't find the most important piece of the puzzle. She wasn't there so I left a message on the answering machine. Why? What's wrong?"

"I think—"

"I brought brownies, too," Faith interrupted them cheerfully, carrying a tray with a pitcher of lemonade and three glasses.

Evie smiled at the girl, glad to see that in spite of the scare they'd had at Sophie's house earlier that morning, she seemed to be fine. Or maybe Rocky had something to do with it. Faith and the puppy had become inseparable.

"Can I show her the rest of the boat now, Sam?" Faith asked hopefully.

"That's up to Evie. She might not have time."

A warm feeling trickled through Evie. Once again Sam was giving her an "out."

He had to be aware of her reaction to the water. And a man whose list of hobbies revolved around it probably wouldn't understand why she was afraid. She didn't quite understand it herself. When Faith suggested a tour of the *Natalie,* Evie had braced herself for a teasing comment or look of amusement from Sam. She'd been shocked when she didn't receive either one. In fact, the expression in his eyes when she'd agreed had stolen the breath from her lungs. It had almost looked like…respect? Affection?

Impossible.

Evie surged to her feet. At that moment, she would have jumped overboard and dog-paddled to Canada if it took her away from Sam's unnerving presence. "I've got time. Let's go."

"This is where I sleep." Faith clattered down the steps and moved to the side so Evie could peek into the tiny room, roughly the same dimensions as Caitlin's walk-in closet! The decor was strictly functional. A narrow bunk covered with a navy spread. A pair of vintage maps in mismatched frames that hung crookedly above a corner desk.

Maps. Fleetingly, she wondered if she'd convinced Sam that they might have the *Noble*'s location. She still didn't know why his gaze had narrowed when she'd told him that she'd shared the information with Sophie. Maybe he thought she should have waited until they were sure so it wouldn't raise Sophie's hopes.

"What do you think?"

Faith's question coaxed Evie back to the moment. "It's cozy." And cramped. But if Evie kept her gaze from drifting out the window, she could almost imagine she was in a studio apartment. Almost.

"That's the desk Sam chains me to so I get my homework done," Faith confided.

"I heard that!" Sam called down from the upper deck.

Faith grinned. "He has ears like a fox."

"I heard that, too."

Evie's heart listed, and this time she couldn't blame the waves. She found herself wishing she could take Faith up on her invitation to spend the rest of the day with them. But the thought of being out on Lake Superior in a boat like the *Natalie* turned her knees to jelly. She'd gotten seasick just watching the boat bump against the dock. Imagine how she'd feel if she actually…

The engine roared to life and Evie clutched the door frame. "What's he doing?"

"Sam always checks everything before we go out," Faith said blithely.

"Oh." Evie felt foolish. Of course he did.

"Come on. I'll show you the kitchen." Faith raised her voice above the gargle and sputter of the engine. She led the way while Evie trailed behind, trying to concentrate on her young guide's knowledgeable monologue about the boat.

The tiny kitchen charmed Evie. Even though there was barely enough room to turn around, it was out-fitted with a sink, stove, refrigerator and a row of open-faced cabinets crowded with a mismatched set of dishes. Someone had added a whimsical touch by stenciling cherries and cherry blossoms along the ceiling, and the colorful rag rug on the floor repeated the bright yellows, greens and reds.

"Look." Faith opened one of the cabinets and proudly pointed to an enormous jar of peanut butter. "Sam lets me do most of the cooking while we're on board, but you can help me if you want to."

"I'm not going to be here for…" The boat pitched to one side and Evie caught her breath. "Wow. For a minute there it felt like the boat was moving."

Faith's eyes widened. "It is."

Sam heard Evie's shriek above the sound of the engine.

Five, four, three, two…

Her feet thumped up the stairs and she appeared in front of him, hands planted on her hips. "What do you think you're doing?"

"Taking you somewhere we can talk." Sam turned the wheel slightly to the left as the *Natalie* chugged cheerfully away from the dock.

The color ebbed from Evie's face, highlighting the constellation of freckles sprinkled across her nose. *All twelve of them.* "We can talk on land."

"This is more private."

"You *planned* this."

"No." Sam liked to think of it as taking advantage of the moment. The minute she'd told him she'd left Sophie a message telling her about the map, he knew he couldn't let her go back to the house alone. And it conveniently solved his dilemma on how to keep tabs on her.

"You attract trouble like a magnet." There. Something a science teacher would understand. "I promised your dad I'd look out for you. This is the only place I can do it."

"Whoever wants the information on the *Noble* got what they were looking for. They'll leave me alone now," Evie argued, keeping her voice low so Faith wouldn't hear them.

"Except for the map. Which you now have."

Evie's mouth opened and closed several times like a beached whitefish. "The only people who know about it are you and Sophie...." Her eyes darkened. "You can't possibly think Sophie had something to do with this. You should have seen her expression when she saw the damage and realized all the records were gone."

She was right. He hadn't seen Sophie's expression. But he'd seen Tyson's.

Guilt had been written all over the guy's face. Forget about innocent until proven guilty. When it came to Evie's safety, Tyson was guilty until proven innocent. Sophie's son or not, Sam didn't trust him.

"Faith will be happy to have someone to bunk with." Sam kept his eyes trained on the water so he wouldn't cave in and take Evie back to shore. "Think of this as a field trip."

"Bunk?" Evie gulped. "I'm not staying over-night on this...*leaky bucket*. You have to take me back. *Now.*"

"We should be able to put a call through to our dads sometime tomorrow. Until then, I'm afraid you're stuck with me. And, just for the record, the *Natalie* doesn't leak."

"This is...*kidnapping*." Her voice stretched thinly. "Sophie isn't going to tell anyone about the map."

He had to be honest with her. "Tyson might."

"Tyson?" The flicker of doubt in her eyes told him that she didn't trust the guy, either. "But he was upset when he saw the den and thought Sophie might have gotten hurt. He even arranged for her to stay with Pastor Wallis and his wife."

"He looked like a kid caught with his hand in the cookie jar." Sam's lips flattened. "I had a little talk with one of the deputies this morning. He recog-nized Tyson right away. He's been making the rounds at the local taverns lately and isn't choosy about the company he keeps. If he's out of a job and trying to support a drug habit, you can bet he's snooped around his mother's house. Maybe listened in on her conversations with your dad. He could have tipped off his so-called friends that Patrick had some interesting information about a sunken ship."

"You think Tyson knows Seth Lansky?" Evie slumped back down into the captain's chair and her purse slid to the deck. "Poor Sophie. When I saw the way Tyson reacted this morning, I hoped it meant he cared about her."

"I think he does." As cynical as Sam could be, the protective way Tyson had hovered around Sophie after the deputies left had seemed genuine. "Part two of my conspiracy theory? The break-in woke Tyson up to the fact that he's in deep with the wrong crowd and that's why he shuttled Sophie to her minister's house for a few days. He wants to keep her out of the way." Just like I'm keeping you out of the way.

As if she'd read his mind, panic flared in Evie's eyes. "If you take me back, I promise I'll check into a hotel."

Sam thought about it. For two seconds. The only way he'd get a good night's sleep was if he knew exactly where Evie was and who she was with. "Sorry."

"I don't have a change of clothes."

"Faith always keeps extra on board. And I have a spare pair of sweats." On cue, an image of Evie, looking adorably rumpled in his rolled-up sweatpants and T-shirt, downloaded into his brain. He shook it away.

"Beach Glass is open tomorrow—I can't just walk away from my responsibility."

"Neither can I."

"I'm not your responsibility." Evie folded her arms across her chest.

"Take that up with Patrick, okay? By this time tomorrow, we'll know if you're right about the map." And he'd find out if he was right about Tyson and Seth

Lansky. And ask the deputy to run a check on Lansky, something he kicked himself for not doing sooner.

"You can't keep me—"

"You changed your mind about coming with us!" With what Sam considered to be an example of perfect timing, Faith rounded the corner and made a beeline to Evie.

And hugged her.

Evie's eyes met Sam's over Faith's shoulder. The smug glint in those smoky depths made her want to push him overboard. Except then no one would be driving the boat. And she'd actually been gullible enough to believe that Sam respected her fear of the water when all along he'd planned to lure her out into the middle of Lake Superior!

Her mouth felt as dry and gritty as the sand on the beach and Evie had to loosen her death grip on the straps of her purse in order to return Faith's impulsive hug.

For Faith's sake, she had to pretend to be a willing captive.

Her gaze shifted from Sam to the passing scenery as the *Natalie* cut a choppy path through the waves, like a pair of dull scissors through satin. The waning afternoon sun coaxed out the deep golds and crimsons etched in the sandstone bluffs, and in the far distance, Evie saw the boxy silhouette of a barge against the horizon.

Hadn't she wished she could be out on the water with Sam and Faith? Watching seagulls coast on the air currents over her head? Feeling the spray of the water against her face?

So not funny, Lord.

"Evie." Sam's husky voice sent shivers down her arms. "Come over here for a minute."

Evie's eyes narrowed suspiciously. "Why?"

"We're going to make you an honorary sailor."

Faith giggled and flopped down on the vinyl-covered bench that curved in a semicircle around the cabin. Evie shot her a look. "Are you an honorary sailor, too?"

"Yup." Faith nodded vigorously.

Sam held out his hand, and Evie automatically grabbed it. He pulled her gently in front of him and curved her fingers over the steering wheel.

"Oh, no." Evie took a step back and bumped into the solid wall of his chest. "Absolutely not."

"You can do it. It's not much different than driving a car."

"Sure. Except for the treacherous underwater reefs."

"Come on, Evie." Faith's eyes sparkled. "Sam's right."

"That's one for the books," he whispered.

Faith wrinkled her nose at her uncle. "I'm going to check on Rocky. I'll be right back."

"She's going to put on a life jacket, isn't she?"

Evie felt Sam's low rumble of laughter down to her

toes. "This should be a piece of cake for a woman who can put together a bomb in a wayside restroom."

"It was a *distraction*."

The movement of the boat had nothing to do with the nervous flutter in Evie's stomach. If she moved a fraction of an inch in any direction, she and Sam would be touching. She swallowed hard, aware of the corded muscles in the forearms braced on either side of her. And the warm strength of his fingers as they moved to cover hers.

She relaxed her grip and watched the blood rush back into her knuckles. She lifted her chin and felt the breeze cup her face and playfully ruffle her hair.

Okay, Lord, maybe this isn't so bad. After all, You created the land and the water and declared both of them good, right?

"It's different, isn't it?" Sam murmured. "To feel the movement of the waves instead of watching them from land. It gives you a whole new perspective."

Evie closed her eyes briefly. He'd not only read her mind, he'd just come close to describing her entire life. And lately she'd started to realize there was a difference between planning every moment of the day and actually living them.

"Hey." The tug of Sam's voice opened her eyes. Evie twisted slightly and looked up him, catching a glimpse of the half smile that tilted the corner of his lips. "Don't hit the island, okay? Rule number one—drive the boat with your eyes *open*."

"I'll remember that. *Captain.*" Evie raised two fingers to her forehead in a mischievous salute.

Sam's eyebrow arched. "Does this mean I'm absolved of all kidnapping charges?"

She tilted her head. "Maybe. But you have to promise me smooth sailing. And a blindfold wouldn't be a bad idea, either."

The breeze caught a few strands of her hair and blew it into her eyes. Before she could move, Sam reached out and tucked them behind her ear. He was so close she could see where the pewter-gray centers of his eyes deepened to charcoal.

Sunspots danced in front of Evie's eyes, and she felt curiously lightheaded. Probably the heat. Where was her straw hat when she needed it?

Sam shifted his gaze to a point somewhere in the distance. "I talked to Rachel before Faith and I left this afternoon."

Chapter Sixteen

"How is Dan?" The fragile thread connecting them gave Evie the courage to ask the question.

"It's not Dan." Sam's exhale stirred her hair. "There's been no change with him. It's Rachel…"

Evie held her breath and waited.

"You have to know Rachel. She's very emotional. Dan is easygoing but in their relationship, he's the strong one. I was afraid Rachel would fall apart when Dan got hurt, but she tried to keep it together for Faith. By the time the hospital moved him to the rehab facility, the stress was getting to her."

"I felt like Dad and I not only bailed on Dan, we bailed on her, too," Sam admitted. "Dan's doctor and the social worker…they didn't come right out and say it, but we were hurting Dan's recovery. He's bitter and angry and doesn't want to see me…us."

The edge of pain in Sam's voice sawed through

Evie's defenses. She couldn't imagine how she'd react if one of her sisters turned her back on the rest of the family and refused to let them help her.

"I check in with Rachel at least once a day. The first few times I talked to her, she couldn't make it through the conversation without crying."

"She's depressed?"

"I was beginning to think so. I even told her the last time we talked that I'd bring Faith back as soon as Dad got home, but today when I talked to her, she sounded...different. Better. She even made a joke about losing weight on the 'cafeteria diet.' I figured her good mood meant Dan was coming around, but when I asked if there was a change, she said no. I can't figure it out."

"Maybe she's decided she has to face whatever happens head-on."

Sam shook his head. "You don't know Rachel. She's not that strong. She has to hold on to someone. I think that's one of the reasons Dan is depressed. He knows how much Rachel depends on him. Now that we're not there, a friend of hers from work has been spending time at the hospital with her. Rachel mentioned she went to church with her this morning."

Evie thought about all the prayers being said on behalf of the Cutter family, and something stirred inside her.

Sam struggled with guilt for leaving Rachel and Dan alone but maybe he *hadn't*. Maybe God had intervened and cleared a work space at the rehab facility. And he'd started with Rachel.

God, You are so incredible.

"Maybe the change isn't in Dan," she offered tentatively, not sure how Sam would respond to her theory. "Maybe it's in *her.*"

"What do you mean?" Sam frowned and adjusted the steering wheel.

"Maybe Rachel let God take over," Evie said simply.

"God?" Sam repeated.

"When you give God control of your life—and your heart—you don't have to muster up strength to make it through the day. He *is* your strength."

Sam stared at her, speechless.

It had to be a coincidence. Sam had taken Evie's advice and thumbed through the book of Psalms when he'd found it lying on Faith's bunk that morning. He had no idea where to start, so he'd randomly picked one out and started reading.

I love you, O Lord, my strength. The Lord is my rock, my fortress and my deliverer; my God is my rock, in whom I take refuge…

Sam hadn't expected the verses to lodge in his brain. Or brand his soul. He'd read the entire passage and remembered thinking that if God was everything a man named David believed Him to be, no wonder he'd loved Him. No wonder he'd turned to Him for help.

No wonder he'd trusted Him.

"So I should just let God take over? Not *do* anything?"

"Yes, you should let God take over. And no, I never said you don't have to *do* anything. The things we're responsible for—trusting, loving, believing—they're all acts of will. And they don't just happen once. We have to keep choosing them. Sometimes day by day. Sometimes second by second. Sometimes breath by breath."

Did he believe her? Evie wished Sam could see her in the classroom, confident and secure with her students, instead of worrying about Patrick and shaking like a leaf after her run-in with Seth Lansky. If she had half of Caitlin's fearlessness and Meghan's moxie, she knew she'd be a better example of someone who wholeheartedly trusted God.

"Hey, Evie!" Faith's muffled voice floated to the top deck. "Can you read through an essay I finished?"

"I'll be right down."

The corner of Sam's lips tipped. "Thanks, Evie."

Evie nodded mutely as she ducked under his arm and went below deck.

Had he thanked her for helping Faith? Or for something else?

"Do you want to help me make supper?" Faith closed her folder and with a twist of her wrist sent it hurtling toward the desk in the corner.

"I'd love to." Evie followed Faith into the kitchen

to survey the well-stocked pantry. "Macaroni and cheese? Or ham sandwiches?"

One of the times she'd gone camping as a child stirred in Evie's memory. "Have you ever made ship-wreck dinner?" she asked, trying not to wince as she said the name. Maybe they could come up with a new one. Like "safe-on-land dinner."

Faith made a face. "It's not raw fish, is it?"

Evie laughed. "I'll have you know that some people pay a lot of money for raw fish. But no, this has nothing to do with fish. We'll need hamburger, onions, carrots and potatoes. And foil."

"Okay. I think we've got all that." Faith gathered the ingredients while Evie kept one ear tuned to the sound of Sam's footsteps on the deck above them. As if by unspoken agreement, they'd given each other some space.

"Are you two ready to go ashore?" Sam called down.

Evie's heart bottomed out. "He's kidding, isn't he?"

"Sometimes we anchor and take the little boat into shore for a few hours."

"The *little* boat?"

"It's fun."

"If you say so."

Faith grinned. "I'll get you a life jacket."

"I look like a cross between the Michelin man and Santa Claus," Evie said, striking a pose in the bulky vest.

Faith giggled. "I think that one is Grandpa's."

"It is." Sam came up behind them. "Let me see what I can do to make it fit better." He yanked on the belt and cinched it tighter around her middle. "Can you breathe?"

No. Not with you so close. "Yes."

"Good." Sam tugged on Faith's jacket and adjusted one of the shoulder straps. "The boat's ready."

Evie peered over the side of the *Natalie* and gulped. The dinghy secured to a line off the *Natalie*'s bow was the size of a bathtub. And the peaceful cove looked *very* far away.

"Faith, you get in first and I'll hand Rocky to you," Sam directed. "Make sure you hold on to him."

"I will." Faith practically skipped down the ladder and reached out to take the puppy.

Evie, not wanting to deal with the raft until absolutely necessary, focused on their destination instead. The cove was a smooth notch carved from the rugged shoreline, its backdrop a canvas of sandstone stained by the iron-rich water that trickled down its surface.

Her gaze traced the curve of the shoreline to the narrow finger of land that pointed to one of the smaller islands. Farther down, Cooper's Landing sprawled at the edge of a stretch of golden sand.

"Evie? Ready?" Sam's husky voice momentarily distracted her.

"Not even close," Evie muttered.

Sam didn't try to take her hand as she turned her

back toward the water, grabbed the rails and settled one foot on the top rung of the ladder.

He smiled down at her. "Don't worry. If you fall in, you'll float."

"That's so comforting." Evie's foot found the next rung. "You should be writing the inside copy of greeting cards."

Sam laughed outright, almost causing Evie to lose her balance. He didn't laugh very often, and this one swept away the shadows that lingered in his eyes, arrowing straight to her heart. "I'll keep that in mind if I ever lose my job."

Evie inched the rest of the way down the ladder, and Faith shifted to make room for her.

The word *sardines* came to Evie's mind as she wriggled into place and watched as Sam practically swung from the deck of the *Natalie* into the boat.

Show-off.

He unhooked the line and Evie linked her arm through Faith's.

"Everyone okay?" Sam asked over the gurgle of the motor.

"Yup," Faith sang out.

Evie was relieved Faith answered the question.

Within minutes, they left the *Natalie* behind and were skipping over the waves toward shore.

"Look! There's another boat." Faith pointed out a boat close in size to the *Natalie,* but the similarity ended there. Its chrome accents gleamed like the edge of a new razor while the sleek lines and onyx finish put it into a completely different league.

Sam's eyes narrowed. "I see it."

He turned the boat to the left and nudged the throttle up another notch. The dinghy agreeably picked up speed.

Evie kept her eyes trained on the speedboat. Was it her imagination or had it changed direction, too? And instead of taking a wide berth around them, it set a course that would put them directly in its path.

"Don't they see us?" Faith asked worriedly.

"I'm sure they do." The grim look on Sam's face belied his reassuring words.

Evie cast a panicked look toward the cove and then at the boat rapidly closing the distance between them. Three-foot waves sloughed off her sides, gliding smoothly toward them like the dorsal fins of a school of sharks.

Sam shot a look at Evie. "Hang on tight. It's going to get bumpy."

Evie sucked in a breath and nodded. She could see people on the deck, but instead of witnessing a frantic effort to give them some space, the crew had lined up at the rail to watch.

To watch what? Their boat capsize?

Faith made a frightened sound and burrowed against Evie's shoulder as a wave slapped the side of the boat and tipped it. Before the boat had a chance to recover, a larger wave slammed against it.

Cold water poured over the side and filled the bottom of the boat.

Evie closed her eyes and began to pray.

She prayed as she ground her feet against the floor of the dinghy and held tightly to Faith. She felt Sam's fingers grip her knee in an effort to keep her from pitching over the side.

Evie didn't open her eyes until the motor quit, and then she wished she hadn't. The sight off the bow squeezed the air out of her lungs. Instead of cruising past them, the black speedboat had cut its engine, too, positioning itself like a guard dog between their tiny boat and the shore.

It was close enough for Evie to read the name *Fury* scrawled across the bow, the red letters painted to resemble flames.

Sam half rose to his feet. "Are you insane?" he shouted at the man who came up to the railing and raised one hand in a casual salute.

"I like to think of it as *committed.*" Seth Lansky grinned at Evie. "I thought it would be rude not to stop and say hello."

Sam wanted to keelhaul Lansky. Not for almost capsizing them but for the leering smile he aimed at Evie.

He moved to shield her from Lansky's view.

Seth looked offended. "What's the matter, Cutter? We're just being neighborly."

"By trying to drown us?" Sam called back irritably.

Seth shrugged. "Sorry. I guess I got a little close."

He was *still* a little too close, but Sam didn't bother to mention that. The waves had settled down into a gentle rocking motion, but they were still in a precarious position. Sam had no idea what Lansky was going to do next. His jovial greeting hadn't fooled Sam for a second. The guy was certifiable and, at the moment, they were sitting ducks.

"It's late in the day to be going out for a pleasure cruise," Seth mused.

"There's plenty of daylight left."

"We're doing some fishing this afternoon," Seth went on pleasantly.

"Good luck with that." Sam decided to dispense with the small talk and kept a wary eye on the *Fury* as he reached down and started the motor. It sounded like a Chihuahua growling at a Doberman, but Seth nodded to the man at the wheel.

The *Fury*'s engine roared to life, and Lansky strolled down the length of the rail, which gave him a bead on Evie again. "Miss McBride? Tell Patrick hello from me. And be sure to mention I'll see him around."

The *Fury* surged away, kicking up another row of waves large enough to swamp them. The little boat valiantly battled its way through them, but even when the water calmed, Sam's heart still hammered against his chest.

He didn't have to wonder anymore if he'd over-reacted by keeping Evie close. If Seth had stolen

Sophie's collection of records about the *Noble,* it meant he was getting desperate to find the location of the ship. And if Sam had to take a wild guess as to what that desperation stemmed from, he'd bet it had something to do with Seth's fear he wouldn't get to it first.

"Why did they do that?" Faith scrambled toward him and Sam caught her against his chest. "And why was Tyson with them?"

"You saw Tyson?" Sam looked at her intently. "Are you sure?"

"I saw him looking out the porthole at us." Faith twisted around. "Didn't you see him, Evie?"

Evie shook her head, but the weary resignation in her eyes told Sam that she believed Faith had.

Sam's stomach knotted. Seth and Tyson. Teamed up and getting antsy. And how was he supposed to tell Sophie that her son had been involved in the break-in at her home?

"Shouldn't we go back to the *Natalie?*" Evie asked quietly. "All our supplies are soaked."

Over her shoulder, Sam watched the *Fury* drop anchor a mere hundred yards from the *Natalie.*

"Let's just stick to our original plan for now."

Evie could have cried with relief when the bottom of the boat finally scraped against a shelf of sand in the shallow water. Their clothing was almost dry, compliments of the wind, and Faith no longer clung to Sam like a barnacle.

Not that Evie blamed her. The stomach-churning boat ride reminded her why she avoided amusement park rides.

Sam rolled up the bottom of his jeans and hopped out of the boat. He reached for Faith, but she gave him an armful of wiggling puppy first. He deposited Rocky on the sand and reached for his niece. As soon as Faith's feet touched dry land, she and Rocky scurried away to explore.

Evie peeled off her shoes and socks and wrung the water from them.

"Sandals are a good choice for the beach." Sam returned, eyeing the dripping socks with that familiar glint of amusement in his eyes.

She was glad he found something humorous about their near-death experience.

Evie stuffed the socks into the toes of her shoes. "You're forgetting one small detail. I wasn't planning to *go* to the beach today. And another thing…your methods of convincing me to *like* the water need some fine-tuning."

Sam's lips twitched. "Really? Because I thought you turned a much lighter shade of green this time." Before she could protest, he reached down and plucked her out of the boat and waded toward shore.

Evie smiled up at him. Which didn't make any sense. After what they'd just been through, and with the *Fury* looming like a specter right off *Natalie*'s stern, the last thing she should feel like doing was laughing. But she did. "That's all right, then. According to Caitlin, green is a good color on me."

"Evangeline McBride, you are…" Sam searched for a word.

Even without a thesaurus handy, Evie could have filled in the blank. *A worrywart*—Caitlin's personal favorite. *Organized*—Meghan's more tactful description. *Capable*—Patrick's loving moniker.

"Amazing."

That simple word would have been enough to render Evie speechless.

But then he kissed her.

Chapter Seventeen

He'd kissed her. Kissed her! And then apologized.
I'm sorry, Evie. I don't know why I did that.

At least afterward, Evie thought wryly, he hadn't asked her for her notes from her first class. The first kiss she'd ever received was from a boy who'd charmed his way through her defenses to bump up his ACT scores.

An hour had passed and she could still feel the warm press of his lips against hers.

Evie groaned silently.

She *couldn't* be falling for Sam.

She had a pretty good idea of the kind of man God would choose for her to spend the rest of her life with. Maybe a fellow teacher. Definitely someone who loved to spend quiet evenings at home and enjoyed home projects...

An image of Sam walking the roofline of the

cabin, his T-shirt casually draped over his shoulder, came to mind. Evie shook it away. Replacing a roof wasn't the kind of home project she had in mind. Gardening. Painting a front door. They had to have some sort of common ground…some of the same interests and hobbies.

But more important, Evie knew her future husband's life had to be centered on Jesus' greatest commandment: *Love the Lord your God with all your heart and with all your soul and with all your mind…and love your neighbor as yourself.*

She sensed Sam's heart softening toward God, but it was obvious an internal battle waged inside him. She could tell he'd really been listening to her after he'd opened up about the change in Rachel, but Evie still didn't know if he'd put his trust in God.

Evie found herself frequently praying for Sam over the course of a day. And not only praying for him. Thinking about him. A lot.

When had she started to care so much?

Sam stalked the perimeter of Evie's personal space for over an hour after they came ashore, trying to figure out the best way to apologize. Because the way she kept avoiding his eyes told him that she hadn't forgiven him. She and Faith stuck together, making a private conversation with her impossible.

It wasn't until Rocky scampered down the beach and Faith chased after him that Sam had an opportunity to approach Evie. He followed the imprint of her shoes in the damp sand to a tangle of driftwood.

"Evie?"

Her shoulders tensed at the sound of his voice, but she didn't turn around. "Faith is doing really well in math. In fact, I think she might even be ahead of her classmates by fall. This week, we'll concentrate on grammar. She's still struggling a little with diagramming sentences, but she's smart. She'll get it."

Sam hadn't followed her to get an update on Faith's progress but the message was clear. *You hired me to be Faith's tutor.*

She put him firmly back in his place and the regret that weighted Sam down took him by surprise. That afternoon, when she'd told him about her sisters, he'd felt the first tenuous threads of *something* between them. And the threads had multiplied again when he'd confided in her about the change in Rachel.

He decided to try again anyway. "I'm—"

"Sorry. I know. You don't have to say it again." Evie sat down on a large piece of driftwood and stared at the horizon.

He didn't? Then why wouldn't she look at him?

Sam pushed his fingers through his hair. Maybe the fact she had to spend the night on the *Natalie* in the shadow of the *Fury* had her upset. "I know you don't like the water and I'm sorry I made it hard for you to go back to Cooper's Landing until tomorrow—" *Now* she looked at him. And it almost burned off the top layer of his skin. *Ouch.* "Okay…I made it *impossible* for you to go back to Cooper's Landing. But after what happened at Sophie's, I have to know you're all right."

"Why?"

The simple question ripped apart his prepared speech. Because she'd gotten under his skin? Because waiting to see what she was going to do next reminded him of trying to keep up with the changing wind currents when he sailed?

"I have no idea. You were just—"

"There. I know."

"No, you *don't* know. You make it sound like I would have kissed anyone," Sam said irritably.

Evie didn't answer.

Was *that* what she thought? That he made a habit of randomly kissing women standing within a five-foot radius?

Sam studied the faint blush of color on her cheeks in disbelief and realized that was *exactly* what she thought.

Maybe some guys' overinflated egos liked the idea of being labeled a "player," but it didn't sit well with Sam. "I don't play games like that," he said flatly. "Ever."

The confusion on Evie's face confused *him.* And then, almost as if someone turned on the proverbial lightbulb in his head, Sam knew. The day he'd told her she had brains and beauty, she'd totally shut down on him. He'd assumed she'd been reacting out of her fatigue, but now he wasn't so sure. Maybe her sudden retreat had been due to her rejection of his compliment.

The logical part of him, the part that was scared to death of giving Evie a weapon she could use against him in the future, urged him to go ahead and let her think he was some kind of Casanova.

But he couldn't do it.

"*You* were the reason I kissed you," Sam told her with quiet force. "You weren't conveniently in range. Or practice. Or a challenge. Or a chalk mark on the board. I kissed you because I'm attracted to you. And to tell you the truth, the only thing I really regret is upsetting you."

He rose to his feet and stared down at her. "Are we clear?"

She nodded mutely.

"Good. I'm going to find some wood to make a fire and try to concentrate on what to do about Lansky instead of kissing you again." Did he say that out loud?

Evie blushed.

Apparently so.

While Sam gathered driftwood for a campfire, Evie coached Faith through the dinner preparations. Which involved wrapping their food in tin foil and burying it in a hole they'd dug in the sand. It helped keep her mind focused on a task instead of Sam's stunning disclosure.

You *were the reason I kissed you.*

He'd stalked away, leaving her alone to sort out her tangled emotions. And to send up several fervent prayers asking for wisdom. She had a feeling she and Sam had just turned a corner. Instead of being nervous, she found herself actually looking forward to what would come next. Which made her more nervous. She didn't even *like* surprises.

"Earth to Evie." Faith waggled a stick in front of her nose. "When can we eat? I'm starving."

"In about an hour." Evie sat back on her heels and retrieved a handful of tiny packets of disposable washcloths from her purse. She peeled one open and wiped the sand off her fingers as Faith peered doubtfully into the makeshift oven.

"Does it really cook in there?"

"It'll be delicious. I promise." Evie handed her one of the packets.

"Who taught you how to make them?"

"My mom. We camped a lot when I was growing up." Funny how she'd forgotten how much time her family had spent camping and hiking through state parks over summer vacation. Laura saved all her vacation days for the months of June, July and August so she was free to travel with them.

Under their parents' watchful eyes, Evie and her sisters had learned how to bait a hook and clean whatever fish they caught. And cook it in the cast-iron skillet over an open fire. They'd also become expert outdoor chefs with gooey homemade "pies" cooked in a special iron and had copied Laura's famous recipe for "shipwreck" dinner.

Evie caught herself smiling. She and Meghan loved to fish but Caitlin hated it. The only way they could get her to join in was to make it a competition to see who could catch the biggest one.

She could still see her mother flipping pancakes on the griddle or rigging up an outdoor shower. During the day Laura brought their attention to wildlife camouflaged by the trees and after the sun set she'd spread out blankets on the ground and point out the constellations as they lay on their backs under the night sky.

Somewhere along the way, Evie had forgotten those summer camping trips that had fostered her love for science. Her mother's passion and enthusiasm had been contagious—and out of the three girls, Evie had been the one who'd wholeheartedly embraced it.

As she let herself think about the past, Evie realized her memories had divided into two categories. "Life Before Mom Died" and "Life After Mom Died." And it occurred to her that she dwelled more on the ones in the second category. In many ways Laura's death had become the defining moment of Evie's life.

That day had drawn an invisible curtain between the past and the future and cast a shadow over the good memories the family had shared. And irrevocably changed how they created new memories.

After the funeral, Evie had made her father promise he'd always be there for her—that he'd take care of himself so nothing would happen to him.

Evie didn't even miss the camping trips the following summer. It would have been too difficult to enjoy them without Laura's presence. Patrick's hobbies changed from rock collecting to collecting antiques at auctions and estate sales. Evie spent her summers reading while Patrick remained close by, restoring vintage furniture to its original charm and then selling it to a local antique store.

Her dad hadn't seemed to mind staying close to home. And he'd kept his promise. Until now. Why had he broken it? Because of Sophie? His friendship with Jacob? Didn't he care that she was worried about him?

"Evie, can I ask you a question?" Faith dragged a path through the sand with the tip of a stick.

Evie took a ragged breath, still shaken by the bittersweet memories. Somehow she'd lost sight of the fact that Laura had been a devoted mother and not just a respected police officer. "Of course you can, sweetheart."

"How old were you when your mom died?"

"Fourteen."

"How did… What happened?"

Pain shot through Evie. It wasn't the question she'd been expecting, but it was the one she'd been dreading since she'd found out Faith's father was a police officer. "She died…at work."

Confusion clouded Faith's eyes. "Was she a teacher like you and your dad?"

Evie knew there was no way around such a direct question. "No. She was a police officer."

"Really? Like my Dad? And Sam?"

"Sam?" Evie's world suddenly tilted. "I thought you said Sam works at a desk all day."

"He does. He's a chief of police."

Sam didn't mean to eavesdrop. He'd gone to get more kindling and when he returned, Faith and Evie didn't hear him come up behind them.

Faith's first tentative question welded his feet to the ground. The second one nearly wrecked him.

Evie's mother had been a police officer? How could Jacob have failed to mention that? He and Patrick had been friends for months—he had to have known.

She died at work.

In the line of duty.

Sam's lungs burned at the pain he saw etched on Evie's face. *Fourteen.* She hadn't been much older than Faith when her mother died.

Because of Dan's injury, he had an idea what Evie's family had gone through. Sam had wrestled with the reality of losing his brother during the long surgery after the shooting. But even though Dan had survived, Sam discovered there were other ways you could lose someone you loved.

Just as he was processing how hard it must have been on Evie, Faith dropped her next question. And Evie's response ripped through him like shrapnel.

She thought he had a *desk* job?

Sam replayed conversations he and Evie had had since they first met and realized she'd never asked him what he did for a living. He'd assumed she knew. Apparently, their dads weren't the doting type that talked about their kids' accomplishments!

His law enforcement career had started at eighteen when he and Dan had applied to the tech school. But their careers had taken different paths. Dan loved being a patrol officer. He thrived in the middle of chaos and enjoyed dealing with the public. He had a reputation for being fair and even-tempered in the community while his zany sense of humor provided comic relief for his fellow officers during the course of a stressful day.

Sam had discovered his strengths rose to the surface while dealing with his peers and taking on roles of leadership within the department. While Dan had passed up promotion after promotion in order to stay on the road, Sam had taken every one they offered him. Eventually, he'd applied and been hired as chief of police in Summer Harbor, a small town in Door County. The rare opportunity to make it to the top of command at the age of thirty had forced him to make some difficult decisions, but he hadn't regretted it. Even when his dedication to his career had meant sacrificing his relationship with his fiancée.

But now Sam realized he must not have loved Kelly at all. Because he hadn't experienced a tenth of the pain when she'd walked out on him as he did now when he saw the look of horror in Evie's eyes.

She'd looked doubtful enough when he'd described his favorite hobbies. There was no way she would willingly accept his choice of career.

Especially a career responsible for taking her mother's life.

Everything suddenly made sense to Evie.

Sam's suspicious attitude when Seth Lansky had wormed his way into her dad's house. His take-charge attitude. His innate confidence. The way he'd reacted at Sophie's.

Evie closed her eyes.

Sam had practically processed the crime scene. The only thing he hadn't done was file a report. He'd asked Sophie the right questions. He'd warned them not to touch anything until the deputies had an opportunity to photograph the damage.

All the signs had pointed to his profession, and she'd been totally blind.

A police chief.

Up until that moment, Evie hadn't known how

deeply her feelings for Sam had taken root. Until Faith's innocent disclosure about what he did for a living had ripped them out.

Chapter Eighteen

Evie wasn't sure what was more frightening: spending the night on the *Natalie* or spending another minute in Sam's company now that she knew what he did for a living.

No, not for a living, she amended. Dentists worked for a living. Lawyers worked for a living. Some people defined their lives by their careers, and some people's careers defined their lives.

Police officers, firefighters, soldiers…all of them fell into the second category. And Evie didn't miss the irony that every one of them put their personal safety at risk.

I guess that's it, God. You closed the door on a relationship with Sam.

At least Evie could be grateful she'd be going home in a week and life would return to normal. No more crazy stories about sunken ships. No more bad guys lurking around the corner. No more water. *No more Sam.*

So why didn't the thought of going back to her routine lift her spirits?

"Evie? Faith is ready for bed. She asked me to send you down to say good-night." Sam materialized beside her, wearing a navy-blue hooded sweatshirt. The department logo printed on the front slapped her with a reminder of what he was.

"Sure." Evie turned from the railing and averted her gaze. She'd managed to make it through supper and the trip back to the *Natalie* without talking directly to him. She could make it one more night. All she had to do was keep her distance....

"Evie? After you say good-night to Faith, can we talk?"

No, no, no.

She didn't want to talk to him. She didn't want to think about him. She didn't want to remember the look in his eyes when he'd told her she was amazing. Right before he'd kissed her.

"Please?"

She gave in. But only because she'd been raised to show good manners. And because there was nowhere on the *Natalie* she could hide. "All right."

Faith scooted over when Evie poked her head in the cabin, an invitation for her to join her on the bunk.

"Is the boat still gone?"

The worry in Faith's eyes told Evie she hadn't

gotten over the scare of being caught in the *Fury*'s wake.

"Long gone." *Please, Lord, let them be long gone.*

Just when Evie had started to think they were going to be sleeping on the beach instead of the *Natalie,* Seth must have decided he'd toyed with them long enough. The *Fury* circled the *Natalie* several times and then roared away, disappearing around the rock peninsula.

Without a word, they'd taken advantage of the window of opportunity and immediately packed up the supplies so they could return to the boat. As quickly as possible. Sam had kept one eye on the peninsula and Evie knew he was wondering, too, if the *Fury* had temporarily anchored there, waiting for them to venture back out onto the lake.

"Why was Tyson with them?"

The question tugged at a loose corner of Evie's frayed emotions. She had no idea what to tell Sophie about her son and his involvement with Seth.

"They must be friends of his."

"I guess so." Faith didn't look convinced. "He's always nice to me when I visit Sophie. Sometimes we watch basketball and he makes hot-fudge sundaes."

That would have surprised Evie if she hadn't witnessed Tyson's reaction to the break-in that morning. And the panic in his eyes when he'd asked Sophie if she'd been hurt. His concern for his mother had seemed genuine but it would still break Sophie's heart to find out Tyson had been the one who had told Seth about the *Noble*.

"Will you pray, Evie?"

Evie answered the unexpected question by taking Faith's hand. For the second time, Faith had unknowingly reminded her how to deal with her turbulent thoughts!

"Dear Lord, thank You for watching over us today. Thank You for calming my fear of the water so I could spend the day with Sam and Faith on the boat. Take care of Patrick and Jacob while they're...away. And Faith's mom and dad. It's hard to be apart from the people we love, Lord, but we trust they're in Your hands. And so are we."

She was about to close the prayer with an "Amen," but Faith took a deep breath and attached her own request.

"And I want to go home, God. Can you do something about that? Thanks."

Evie reached out and pulled the blanket up, tucking it around Faith's shoulders as she asked God to answer Faith's heartfelt, innocent prayer.

"Are you coming back soon?" Faith murmured drowsily.

They'd fashioned a mattress for Evie on the floor next to Faith's bunk from the extra blankets on board. Sam had folded one of his sweatshirts to make a pillow.

Practical. And thoughtful. Sam had proven

himself to be both on so many levels since she'd gotten to know him.

"In a few minutes." She wouldn't spend any more time in Sam's company than absolutely necessary. "Sweet dreams."

"You, too."

The fragrant night breeze flowed over Evie as she made her way to the upper deck. Sam stood at the railing, his face tipped toward the sky. Pensive and...vulnerable.

The powerful rush of emotions that rolled through her reminded her of their hair-raising afternoon boat ride. She found it easier to guard her heart when Sam bossed her around, but it wasn't as easy when she caught glimpses of the sensitive man beneath the surface.

"It makes you feel pretty insignificant, doesn't it?" Sam asked without looking at her.

Even as a voice in her head warned her to keep her distance, Evie's feet moved on their own to join him at the railing. "No. Just the opposite. It makes me feel valued. And very...grateful."

"Grateful?" Sam slanted a look at her.

She didn't want to be near Sam, but she couldn't walk away from him when he was obviously searching. And just like Patrick's treasure map, she knew exactly where Sam could find the truth. She couldn't keep that to herself. If Sam was willing to listen, she had to be brave enough to talk.

"Because He not only created me, He loves me. When I look at those stars, I don't think about how small I am, I think about how *big* God is. And how much I mean to Him."

Sam didn't respond, and Evie was torn between wanting to say more and letting God fill the silence.

"Good night, Sam." She decided to let God take over.

Or maybe, Evie thought as she turned away, she was simply too much of a coward to stay any longer.

Sam watched Evie walk away, and it took every ounce of strength not to ask her to come back.

It was a good thing his officers weren't around to witness their chief totally losing his nerve.

He'd wanted to tell Evie he'd overheard her conversation with Faith. He wanted to talk to her about her mother and tell her he understood she fussed over Patrick because she didn't want to lose another parent.

He wanted to tell her he worked in a sleepy town not much bigger than Cooper's Landing. He'd leave out the part about living in a turn-of-the-century lighthouse only a stone's throw from Lake Michigan, but he could honestly tell her the most notorious crime his officers had solved was who'd put Jed Carson's VW Bug on the sidewalk on New Year's Eve.

But deep down, Sam knew none of that would matter to Evie. Whether he lived in a small town or a large city, police work always courted danger. The child of a cop, especially someone with firsthand experience of what the cost could be, knew it was the nature of the job.

Even if he told Evie what his life was like, there was no way he could convince her to embrace it. Or even to accept it.

And he had to face to truth. He *wanted* her to accept it.

Evie was a remarkable woman. Funny. Giving. Insightful. Patient. Beautiful. The kind of woman a man could imagine spending his life with. He'd started out thinking he had to protect her but somehow she'd become his *partner.* Watching out for Faith. Encouraging him to look outside of himself for strength. Facing her fears instead of running away from them. Finding humor in stressful situations.

Sam shook a blanket out and laid it on the deck. He wasn't going to sleep in his cabin and give Lansky another shot at them during the night. He stretched out on his back and folded his arms behind his head, staring up at the stars. The ones that made him feel insignificant and Evie, valued.

He didn't want to accept that the feelings stirring between him and Evie weren't as strong as their differences.

The engine wouldn't start.

Sam had planned to leave for shore right after breakfast, but the *Natalie* had a different agenda.

"Why did you decide right now to go temperamental on me?" Sam muttered, digging in the toolbox for a wrench.

Evie appeared in the doorway, looking annoyingly fresh in the wrinkle-proof khakis she'd worn the day before and Faith's favorite basketball jersey. "What's going on?"

"Something's wrong with the engine."

Evie moved closer to the engine compartment and watched him check the fluids. For the third time. Not that he was a slouch when it came to engines, but the *Natalie* had been around a lot longer than he had.

"It looks like the tube near the bottom is cracked," Evie said.

Sam couldn't believe he'd missed it. "That does pose a problem."

"You must have a backup motor on a boat like this."

"The key words are *on a boat like this.*"

"No backup motor?" Evie frowned.

Sam searched for the roll of duct tape every man stashed in his toolbox. Apparently every man *except* his dad. "Do I smell sausage?"

"Faith is making breakfast. Are you trying to get rid of me?"

"Not if you have something to fix this."

"I'll be right back."

Sam sat back on his heels and waited for her to return. When she did, it was with a roll of duct tape.

"You carry that around in your purse?" Sam saw

her expression and rephrased the question. "Thank you for carrying that around in your purse."

Evie gifted him with a small smile and some of the tension between them dissolved. "Why don't you let me try. My fingers are smaller."

"Be my guest." He regretted the decision as soon as she knelt beside him and the pleasing scent of maple syrup combined with Evie's favorite brand of perfume played havoc with his senses.

"There. That should hold. I'll stay here while you give it a try."

He took advantage of the escape route she'd offered and went on deck. A few seconds later, the engine came to life and Evie clamored up the steps. "It's working!"

"We make a good team," he said without thinking.

Shadows skimmed through Evie's eyes and she backed away. "I'm going to help Faith with breakfast. It's almost ready."

Regret pierced him.

Or not.

Within an hour, Evie's feet touched dry land again. And she wished she was back on the *Natalie* with Sam.

You are out of your mind, Evangeline Elizabeth. You don't like the water. And you can't like Sam.

But she did. That was the problem. In fact, she had nothing to compare her feelings to, but she wondered uneasily if they'd moved past "like."

"Evie?" Sam caught up to her as she hiked through the sand toward her car. "I'm going to stop by and talk to Sophie. Will you come with me?"

Was he asking because he needed her help or because he wanted to keep an eye on her?

"Yes." No matter how anxious Evie was to put some distance between her and Sam, she wanted to be there for Sophie.

"Do you know where her pastor lives?" Sam's expression closed, reminding her of the man who'd come to her door the night she'd met him and told her Faith needed a tutor. A man whose career forced him to ignore his emotions while he helped people deal with theirs during difficult circumstances.

"In a house right behind the church."

"Good." Sam nodded curtly. "Let's go."

Pastor Wallis met them at the front door of the parsonage, dressed casually in twill shorts and a white polo. Only in his midthirties, his approachable manner and compassionate eyes seemed to have a way of immediately putting people at ease. Evie had liked him from the moment her father had introduced them when she'd attended Sunday-morning worship services the summer before.

"Hello, Evie." Pastor Wallis's lively brown eyes lit with a smile that encompassed both of them. "It's good to see you again. I'm sorry I didn't get a chance to chat with you yesterday after the service."

"That's all right." Evie had noticed he was in deep conversation with several teenagers and hadn't wanted to interrupt. "Pastor Wallis, this is Sam Cutter."

"It's nice to meet you." Pastor Wallis extended his hand and gave Sam's a vigorous shake. "Would you like to come in? Barbara took an angel food cake out of the oven a few minutes ago."

"Actually, we're here to see Sophie."

Pastor Wallis frowned. "She's not here. Her son and his friend picked her up early this morning."

"But I thought she planned to stay for a few days." Evie's heart picked up speed.

"She did." The minister frowned. "But after she talked to Tyson, she packed up her things and told us she had to leave. To tell you the truth, Barbara and I both thought Sophie seemed upset. I was planning to call her this evening."

"Did you recognize Tyson's friend?" Sam asked tersely.

Pastor Wallis shook his head. "He didn't get out of the car. I only saw him from the window, and he was looking the other way. Sophie told us about her house getting broken into. Do you think something else happened?"

Evie and Sam exchanged a glance. "We'll stop by her house and make sure she's all right."

"I'd appreciate that."

Sam was already turning away but Evie hesitated.

"Pastor, could we ask a favor? Sam's niece, Faith, is in the car. Is it all right if she stays here for an hour or so?"

The man's eyes lit with understanding. "Of course. My daughter, Samantha, would love the company. She's been complaining since school let out that there's nothing to do around here."

"She must be a teenager." Sam's guess brought a smile to the minister's face.

"She's thirteen."

"I'll get Faith," Evie said quickly. "And Rocky."

"That's right. We have one of Sophie's puppies with us." Sam winced.

"Not a problem. Samantha loves dogs. Bring them both in. I'll tell my two favorite girls we have company."

Faith was hesitant to stay with the Wallis family until Samantha Wallis ran outside, a soccer ball tucked under her arm.

Within minutes Faith waved a cheerful goodbye and the two girls disappeared around the corner of the house.

"That was a good idea until we know everything is okay with Sophie," Sam said. "I didn't even think about what we might be getting Faith into."

Evie tried to ignore the warm glow his words stoked in her heart. "I remembered they have a daughter close to Faith's age. Do you think Seth Lansky was the one with Tyson?" Evie murmured as they hurried back to the car. "Sophie will recognize his name if Tyson introduces them."

"I hope it wasn't him." Sam paused to open the car door for her before moving around to the driver's side. "I changed my mind about needing you to come with me. Do you mind if I drop you off at your house before I go to Sophie's?"

"Yes."

"Good. I'll—"

"Yes, I mind, not yes, you can drop me off. I'm going along."

Sam's lips flat-lined but he didn't argue. Until they got to Sophie's house. He stopped the car before the turn in the driveway and cut the engine.

"Do you mind waiting here for a minute?"

"Yes."

He flashed an impatient look at her. "Is that yes, you'll wait here or yes, you *mind* waiting here?"

"Yes, I mind waiting."

Sam's eyes narrowed. "Evie, I know what I'm doing and I won't be able to concentrate if you're with me. Please stay here while I evaluate the situation."

And let me do my job.

The words he didn't say hung in the air between them. Of course. Sam wasn't planning to walk up to the door and ring the bell.

Evie hesitated, not wanting him to go alone but not wanting to distract him, either. "I'll stay here." And pray.

Now he smiled at her grudging tone. "I'll be right back."

She watched as he melted into the trees instead of walking up the driveway.

As the minutes ticked by, Evie grew more concerned. Why wasn't he back yet?

Sam, where are you?

Lord, please let him be all right.

The two thoughts collided as Evie slipped out of the car and followed the path he'd taken into the woods until the house came into view.

No sign of Sam. Or Sophie.

Evie's heart picked up speed as she stepped out into the open and crossed the bright green patch of yard. Should she knock? Or just go in?

As she hesitated on the porch, a hand grasped her arm. "Sam? Thank goodness. I was starting to get—"

Her voice died in her throat as she saw the bruised and bloody face of the man holding on to her.

Chapter Nineteen

"*Dad!*" Evie's knees turned to water.

"Hi, sweetheart." Patrick smiled wanly and then swayed on his feet.

Evie instinctively caught her dad before he fell over, and her frantic gaze skittered over him. Blood congealed over one eye and angry red scratches crisscrossed his cheek. His muddy clothing hung loosely on his frame and she noticed his glasses were missing. "What happened? Where's Sam? Who did—"

The door flew open.

"Evie." Tyson stepped to the side and motioned for them to come inside. "Come and join the party."

She found her voice and turned on Tyson, anger over Patrick's condition overriding her fear of Sophie's son. "What did you do to him?"

Tyson ignored the question. "Let's go into the kitchen."

Where he kept the knives? Not a chance.

Evie balked and Tyson made an impatient sound. Without ceremony, he nudged her away from her father and wrapped his arm around Patrick's waist.

"Let go of him." She glared at Tyson.

"It's okay, Evie," Patrick murmured.

Evie would have chosen a better word to describe the situation but because she couldn't exactly play tug-of-war with Tyson—with her dad in the middle— she gave in and followed him into the kitchen.

She took a silent inventory of the contents of her purse. If she could get to the travel-size can of hair spray in her bag, she could aim it in Tyson's face and get Patrick safely to the car. And then she could double back to find Sam...

"Oh, good, you found her, Patrick. Hello, Evie."

Evie blinked. Like watching a movie playing in slow motion, she tried to process the scene in front of her. Sophie stood near the kitchen table, calmly dabbing a washcloth against a jagged cut on Jacob Cutter's forehead while Sam knelt on the floor, holding a bag of frozen peas against his father's swollen ankle.

Sam glanced up and gave her a wry look. "I knew you wouldn't stay put."

Evie's face whitened alarmingly and Sam rose to his feet. His dad's sprained ankle could wait.

"Hey. It's okay." Sam drew Evie into his arms and she buried her face in his neck.

"I think we can take him," she whispered in his ear.

Sam choked back a laugh and felt Evie stiffen. "We don't have to take him," he murmured. "He's on our side."

"He's right, Evangeline," Patrick chimed in, wincing as Sophie turned her gentle ministrations to the scratches marking his face.

"But Tyson and Seth Lansky—"

Tyson hooked his foot around a chair, yanked it away from the table and dropped into it. "I can see I'm going to have to go over this one more time."

Sophie gave her son an affectionate smile. "I don't mind hearing it again."

Sam would have steered Evie toward a chair, too, but she took a protective stance near her father.

He didn't blame her. When he'd walked into the house and heard his dad and Sophie arguing over whether or not he needed stitches, he'd been ready to take Tyson apart, too.

And Tyson must have known it because he'd put the table between them while Sophie had intervened and explained the situation.

"It seems Tyson has a gambling problem," Jacob said, a little too jovially in Sam's opinion. "And he made some stupid mistakes. Go ahead and tell her, Ty."

Tyson didn't refute the accusation as he looked at Evie. "He's right. I needed money to pay off a loan from my friend, Gil. I heard Mom and Patrick talking about a sunken ship and I didn't pay much attention at first because I figured it was part of the boring genealogy stuff she's been researching. But when Mom said something about a ring, I got to thinking maybe there was something valuable on board.

"I was at the tavern one night and Gil started hassling me. Anyway, I'd had too much to drink and told him to be patient—that I was going to score some big money. But when I told him about the ship, he laughed and called me a stupid drunk. But the next day a guy called. Said he was a diver and maybe we could help each other out if I could tell him where the *Noble* went down. I did some snooping around here but couldn't find anything. I listened in on Mom's phone conversation and that's when I knew Mom had given Patrick the stuff about the ship." He drummed his fingers against the table and slanted a look at Evie. "I didn't think *she'd* be hard to get past. Seth was supposed to get the information off Patrick's computer without her knowing about it."

"But Sam came to her rescue." Jacob winked at Evie and her eyes widened. "That's part of his job, you know. Rescuing damsels in distress."

Sam groaned inwardly.

Dad, you are so not helping me here.

"Oh, I think Seth found out that Evie's pretty resourceful," Sam mused. "She's good at creating distractions."

There was a moment of silence as everyone in the room looked at Evie. But none of them looked the least bit surprised at his announcement. That seemed to fluster Evie more than anything else, and Sam smiled in satisfaction.

It was obvious from the expression on Tyson's face that he knew about it, too. With an encouraging nod from Patrick, Tyson continued. "When Seth didn't have any luck getting the stuff from Evie, he kept pushing me to find out if Mom had it. But I stalled, thinking Jacob and Patrick would get back and he'd leave her alone and focus on them."

"Tyson is sure Seth is the one who broke in." Sophie picked up the thread of the story calmly, as if she'd already forgotten the trauma of finding her den torn apart and months of precious research missing.

Sam couldn't quite understand that level of forgiveness but he was pretty certain it had something to do with a mother's unconditional love. And maybe her unshakeable faith.

"But I didn't have anything to do with that. I didn't know you'd locked the records in your desk. Seth took a chance and ended up finding them." Tyson looked quickly at Sophie, who smiled reassuringly at him. "I confronted him about it and he threatened me. Said he paid Gil off and now I owed *him*. He'd been watching Evie and was pretty sure she knew about the ship. When she got on the boat with Cutter yesterday, he thought they were going to the wreck site. So we followed you," he added, looking at Evie.

"And almost capsized the boat," Evie reminded him.

Tyson squirmed in the chair but didn't look away. "Yeah. But I didn't know he was going to do that. The guy's crazy, man."

"When Tyson got here, he found Jacob and I camped out in the driveway," Patrick said. "I wanted Sophie to patch me up before I came home, but Tyson told us you were on the boat. Jacob and Tyson picked up Sophie at the Wallis's and brought her home."

"Then we all sat down and had a little talk." Jacob leveled a mock scowl at Tyson.

"I don't care what Lansky does to me," Tyson said in a low voice. "I don't want anyone to get hurt."

"It looks like two people got hurt." Evie's fingers closed over her father's shoulder.

"Oh, Seth Lansky didn't do this, sweetheart." Patrick patted her hand. "It was Bruce Mullins."

Sam pulled out a chair and Evie slid bonelessly into it. Without a word, he poured her a cup of coffee and pushed it in front of her. He'd heard the hasty summary of Tyson's involvement with Seth, but he hadn't heard this part of the story yet.

"This is where things get interesting." Jacob looked smug. "Mullins double-crossed us. We figured it out after we got to the lodge—that's why Patty called Sam and told him to look out for Evie. We asked Bruce questions about how to go about filing for permits and organizing the dive, but he started pumping us for information about where she'd gone down. Got kind of cranky when we wouldn't tell him, too, right, Patrick?"

"Yup. Cranky." Patrick's split lip curved into a smile.

"He wanted to find the *Noble* and file for salvage permits before we had a chance to?" Sophie asked.

"Permits?" Patrick sighed. "We can't prove it, but we doubt they were going to bother waiting around for permits. I think the plan was to salvage the ship before *we* filed for them. We would have followed the rules and come up with a big empty nothing because they'd have gotten to it first."

"But I thought you and Bruce were friends," Evie said in confusion.

Jacob snorted. "So did I. But when you say the word *treasure,* men can get greedy."

"Seth mentioned Bruce Mullins's name once when he was talking about a dive he'd gone on near White-fish Bay," Tyson said. "It didn't mean anything to me at the time, though."

"When Tyson told us about Lansky, we figured Bruce had sent him to nose around here," Patrick added. "Seth got lucky when Tyson's friend started making fun of him and his so-called treasure. We think Bruce's plan was to stall us until Seth had a chance to find out where the *Noble* went down, but he probably started to get impatient, thinking Sam and Evie would team up and go ahead with the search. We think he told Lansky to apply a little pressure."

"On Friday night, we waited until Bruce fell asleep and then we left. We spent the weekend trying to dodge him while we hiked back to the lodge. No tents. No food. Just the clothes on our backs, hey, Patrick?" Jacob reached out and cuffed Patrick's shoulder. "We were starting to worry about what was happening on the home front. Thought maybe you'd need our help."

The two men grinned at each other.

Sam saw Evie's expression. *Uh-oh.*

"Do you mean to tell me…" Evie said in a deceptively pleasant voice "…that you were lost in the woods for two days?"

"Not lost, Evangeline. We had the miniature compass you pinned to the pocket of my shirt," Patrick said.

It didn't look like Evie cared about the compass.

"No food. No tent. Just the clothes on your backs," Evie repeated.

"And we had a great time." Jacob lifted his coffee cup and bumped it against Patrick's.

"A great time," Patrick echoed. "I'd say all in all, the fishing trip was successful."

"What are you talking about?" Evie asked, exasperated. "We all know you didn't go fishing."

"Oh, your dad went fishing, all right," Jacob said wryly. "Fishing for men as the Good Book says. If it hadn't been for Mullins's double cross, I would have thought Patty planned the whole thing."

Sam tensed. *The Good Book?*

"Never underestimate what God will use to get a man's attention." A glint of humor brightened

Patrick's eyes. "All He had to do was get us alone in the wilderness with no food or water…and a sprained ankle…and Mullins hot on our trail…to get this stubborn guy to listen."

"Well, I listened, didn't I?" Jacob said irritably. "Some of us take more convincing than others."

"It has a lot to do with the thickness of the skull." Patrick tapped his index finger against his temple.

"Dad, what are you saying?" Because it couldn't possibly mean what Sam thought it meant.

"I accepted Jesus as my savior. Got my life right with God out there in the woods." He looked at Patrick. "Is that how you say it, Patty?"

Patrick's eyes misted. "That'll do."

Jacob looked at Sam and laughed. "You look a little befuddled, son. I'll tell you all about it. And then, I'd like you and Faith to go back to Chicago with me. 'Cause your brother needs to hear it, too."

"I'm sorry I got you involved in this, Evie."

Evie stiffened when she heard her father's voice behind her. Under protest, he'd agreed to rest for a few hours at home before they met everyone again at Sophie's later. But when they got back to the house, Patrick hadn't rested. Instead, he'd printed out copies of Sophie's documents—something Evie had planned to do before Sam kidnapped her.

"I don't understand why *you* got involved." Evie still winced every time she saw the scratches on his face. Sophie had bandaged the cut over his eye but he still looked like a prize fighter who'd made it to the last round. "You promised—"

She caught herself. She hadn't meant to bring it up now that Patrick was home safe and sound. But she intended to make sure he stayed that way!

Patrick sighed. "The promise I made. I'm sorry—"

"It's okay, Dad. I forgive you."

Patrick gave her a gentle smile. "I'm not sorry I broke it, sweetheart. I'm sorry I made it in the first place."

"What?" Evie choked.

"I shouldn't have made a promise I couldn't keep, but you were young and we'd just lost your mother. I would have done anything to give you the security you needed. I said I'd never do anything that might take me away from you—even though I know our times are in God's hands—and that was wrong. Not only for you, but for me. I gave up things I loved because I didn't want to upset you…but I got restless after I retired. Your mother's been gone a long time but I found myself missing her more than ever. I needed some excitement. Something to make me feel alive again.

"When I met Sophie and she told me about her family genealogy and the scandal with Matthew Graham after the *Noble* sank, it gave me an opportunity to do something that mattered. Instead of selling people bits of the past, I could actually help Sophie connect with hers. She might have told you the search for her family history gave her a reason to live, but it gave me one, too."

Evie was speechless. She hadn't meant the promise to prevent her dad from enjoying life…or to make him give up things he loved, even if they were a little risky. She'd given them up, too. But she hadn't felt the void until she'd spent the day on the *Natalie* and relived the sweet memories of taking camping trips with her family.

She'd never known her father hadn't been as successful as her at forgetting those times. Or that he'd felt as though something were missing.

"Dad, I—"

Patrick held up his hand. "Just hear me out for a minute. Your mother was an amazing woman and I was blessed to have the years together that we did. Laura had a way of turning the most ordinary moments into adventures. She lived fearlessly and generously and she loved us the same way. I wouldn't have changed anything about her. Not even her choice of a career." Patrick gave Evie a tender smile. "You may think you and I are alike, Evangeline, but out of you three girls, *you* remind me the most of your mother. You're smart and curious and you care about people. Laura was that way, too."

All along, Evie realized with sudden, painful clarity, she'd been shaped by her mother's death instead of her life. And her father was right. Laura

McBride had been an amazing woman. A dedicated police officer. And a loving mother.

"Some things are worth the risk." Patrick looked at her intently. "Friendship. Love."

Evie managed a smile as her heart struggled to recognize the truth she'd just discovered. "You love Sophie."

"Jacob loves Sophie," Patrick astounded her by saying. "And she loves him." He chuckled. "And he just might end up being worthy of her after all."

"Jacob and Sophie? Are you all right with that?" Unexpected tears welled up in Evie's eyes. She'd come to love Sophie, and she'd been ready and willing to welcome her into the McBride family.

"Oh, I'm more than all right with it. I've been asking God for months to give two people I care about a second chance at happiness."

Evie's lips parted. And no sound came out. She couldn't see Sophie and Jacob together. Sophie was deep and insightful. Jacob Cutter was, well, *Jacob Cutter.*

"They remind me a little of your mother and I," Patrick went on. "Different, but we brought out the best in each other."

Evie forced her mind to take a detour around thoughts of Sam. She couldn't let herself think about him right now. "Is all this talk about adventure your way of letting me know you're not giving up on the *Noble?*"

"Absolutely. And from what Sam told me, it seems I sent the map to the right McBride daughter."

"I was right?" Evie was momentarily distracted. "That *was* the map showing where the *Noble* sank?"

Patrick smiled in satisfaction. "I knew you'd figure it out and that you'd keep it safe. But now that I'm back, the rest of us can take over from here."

"You're really going to look for the ship?"

"We can't give up now. We have to get everything in order so we can hire a dive team to go down and see if Lady Carrington's dowry is still there. Prove that Matthew wasn't a thief."

"But what about Seth?" Evie asked helplessly. "You know he can't be trusted. And he's still lurking around somewhere, watching you."

"We've got some ideas. That's why we're meeting at Sophie's later. To have a planning session. But you don't have to come along, Evie. You're probably exhausted." Patrick's eyes twinkled as he hobbled away, rubbing the hip that had collided with a tree stump.

"I'll come along," Evie said grimly. "Planning sessions happen to be my specialty."

And, she thought with an aching heart, it might be her last opportunity to say goodbye to Sam.

Chapter Twenty

"God answered my prayer, Evie. I'm going back to Chicago with Grandpa and Sam tomorrow."

Tomorrow?

Faith's exuberant greeting pierced Evie's heart but she reached out and hugged her. "That's great news."

"Grandpa called Dad and I got to talk to him. I told him about Rocky and sleeping on the boat," Faith went on. "And I told him about you, too. He said to tell you thank-you for helping me with my homework. And for playing basketball with me."

Evie tried to swallow around the knot in her throat as Faith towed her toward the people sitting around the crackling bonfire in Sophie's backyard. Jacob and Sophie sat shoulder to shoulder, toasting marshmallows over the glowing embers, while Tyson stood several feet away from them, sharpening the end of a stick with his pocketknife.

For some reason, the homey scene brought tears to her eyes. Maybe her dad was right about Sophie and Jacob being good for each other. And for Tyson.

Evie's gaze swept the yard but there was no sign of Sam anywhere.

"Sam didn't come," Faith told her, as if she knew who Evie was looking for. "He said he had too much packing to do if we're leaving tomorrow. He had to cover the boat and stuff like that."

Sam wasn't going to say goodbye?

Evie bit down on her lip to keep it from trembling. He'd barely spoken to her after he and Jacob had returned from their "talk" but she'd assumed it was because he was still in shock over his father's unexpected announcement. *She* could hardly comprehend that Jacob Cutter had surrendered his life to the Lord. She didn't know what it would mean for Sam and his brother, but she had a feeling that God had separated the entire Cutter family so He could work on them one at a time!

"Evie." Sophie rose to her feet and greeted her with a warm hug. "I was hoping you'd come over this evening with your father. Even though it might be kind of boring talking permits—"

"And strategy." Jacob chortled. "Tyson may have to pretend to be on Lansky's side for another few weeks so we can keep an eye on him and see what he's up to."

That sounded a little dangerous to Evie, but she

saw the first real smile she'd ever seen on Tyson's face. "Boring? Are you kidding? Count me in."

Evie took a deep breath. "Me, too."

"Are you sure, sweetheart?" Patrick came up and linked his arm through hers. "I don't want to take up any more of your summer—you said you had plans."

Plans. Yes, she did have plans. To paint her front door and read through a stack of books. And do some gardening. And she fully intended to check off every one of those things on her list...

After they found the *Noble*.

"Special delivery for Evangeline McBride."

Evie heard the mischievous tone in her father's voice and set aside the box of china she'd been unpacking.

"I hope it's iced tea because I'm—" Her voice trailed off when she saw the huge bouquet of summer flowers in Patrick's arm. Daisies. Roses. Snap dragons. Lavender. All nestled together in a cloud of airy white tulle. "Where did those come from?"

"A florist, I suppose." Patrick smiled at her. "A deliveryman just brought them to the house." He transferred them into her waiting arms and Evie buried her face in the scented blooms.

"There's a card."

"I know." But she didn't want to read it. Already tears clawed at the backs of her eyes. It had been almost a month since the Cutters had left. She knew

Patrick and Jacob kept in contact, but it was as if Sam Cutter had disappeared off the face of the earth.

Or maybe just from your life.

And hadn't she wanted it that way? There couldn't be a future for her and Sam. It was one thing to venture beyond the perimeters she'd put around her life, another to deliberately risk her heart by starting a relationship with a police officer. That was something she didn't think she'd ever be ready for.

"Why don't you put those in some water and I'll finish unpacking the boxes?"

Maybe the flowers weren't from Sam. Maybe Caitlin had sent them as a guilt offering for not being able to visit over the Fourth of July. Or Meghan. Sometimes she did things like send flowers or chocolates for no particular reason other than to "celebrate the day" as she called it.

Evie walked up to the house and let herself inside through the patio door. Vase first. Card later. She carefully unwrapped the filmy netting and the layer of tissue paper underneath it. The tiny linen envelope fell out, drifting gracefully to the table. Reminding her it was there.

"I'll get to you in a minute."

She put the flowers in water and took her time arranging them in an ironstone vase. And then she wiped up the table and rinsed out the dishcloth.

With fingers that shook, she finally tore open the envelope and pulled out the small square of paper inside.

Therefore, if anyone is in Christ, he is a new creation; the old has gone, the new has come!—
2 Corinthians 5:17

Evie sagged against the counter as she stared at the signatures.

Jacob	Rachel
Dan	Faith

And Sam.

In the same tidy script he'd used to sign his name were two more words. *Thank you.*

Overwhelmed, Evie sagged against the counter.

All of them, Lord?

And then she burst into tears.

"He's a good man, Evie." Patrick draped her cardigan around her shoulders and settled down on the dock beside her.

"I know." Evie's gaze didn't shift away from the deep blue seam where the water met the sky in the distance.

Shortly after reading the card, she'd driven to Cooper's Landing and walked to the end of the dock. The *Natalie,* preening in a bright yellow canvas cover, bobbed a greeting. For a minute, she'd let herself remember the strength in Sam's hands as they'd covered hers while she steered the boat out of the harbor.

"Did I imagine it, or was there something happening between you and Sam?"

Something she'd walked away from. Evie drew a careful breath. "We're too different, Dad."

"Are you sure that's the real reason?"

She should have known her father would see through to the truth. "I was too young to realize how dangerous Mom's job was until she didn't come home that day, but now I do *know.* And I can't do it." Evie twisted her fingers together in her lap. "God brought me to Cooper's Landing to help Faith. I'm happy Sam is a Christian now but that doesn't mean we're meant to be together."

"I love you to pieces, Evie, but ever since your mother died you've tried to cocoon yourself from anything that might be painful. And I know I'm partially to blame for going along with it. You won't even go barefoot on the beach."

"That's because there might be broken glass in the sand," Evie muttered in her own defense.

Patrick smiled gently. "The last few weeks, I've seen changes in you. Good ones. And I'd like you to consider something. Maybe God didn't bring you here for Faith and Sam. Maybe He brought Faith and Sam here for *you.*"

Tears spilled down her cheeks. "It might be too late, Dad. He didn't even say goodbye."

Patrick patted her knee. "Maybe because he hoped it wouldn't be."

"Hey, Chief. Mrs. Mattson called and wants us to check out a suspicious truck parked outside her house again."

Sam's chair creaked in protest as he leaned back. "Does this one happen to have the words FedEx printed on the side, too?"

Officer Tony Faller laughed. "I don't know. But I'll take care of it."

"Let me." Sam rose to his feet, once again battling a familiar restlessness that had dogged him the past few weeks. "I could use a change of scenery from the city budget right about now."

"Yeah." Tony made a face. "Sorry about that. It was one thing watching over the town, another one taking on the city council and all those numbers. All I can say is I'm glad you're back."

"You did a great job. At least now I know I can take a leave of absence if necessary." Sam suppressed a smile when he saw the panic in Tony's eyes, but he couldn't help giving the officer a hard time.

Tony had been employed at the Summer Harbor P.D. for only three years, and the mayor had questioned Sam's choice of men to take his place during the month he was in Cooper's Landing. But Sam had pushed and eventually got his way. In personality and dedication, Tony reminded Sam of Dan.

Thanks, Lord.

Every time his brother came to mind, it was the only thing Sam could say. Two simple words, but they came from the depths of his soul.

He still couldn't believe the changes in his family. In a lot of ways, he felt like Dan. Like he was starting from scratch. What had Evie said? Moment by moment? Breath by breath? He hadn't understood what she meant at the time. But now he did.

A hundred times over the past few weeks, he'd wanted to call Evie and fill her in on Dan's progress. But she hadn't made any attempt to contact him since he'd left Cooper's Landing, and that told him, more than anything, exactly where they stood.

Apart.

Even after he'd sent her a bouquet of flowers, she hadn't called or sent a note.

After that, he carefully avoided asking questions about Evie when Jacob called. He knew that, thanks to Tyson, Seth Lansky was being formally charged for possession of stolen property, while Bruce Mullins claimed Seth had acted entirely on his own. Sam even heard subtle references to Jacob's budding romance with Sophie. But Jacob didn't mention Evie, and Sam assumed she'd gone home, as planned.

It was clear that even though they now shared the same faith, Evie didn't see them sharing anything else.

"Not even a pizza," Sam muttered.

"You want to order a pizza?"

"No." He and Tony were friends but he wasn't ready to talk about Evie yet. "I was talking to myself."

"Michelle says you've been doing that a lot lately," Tony said, a glint in his eyes.

"Really?" Sam stalked toward the door, careful not to open it so quickly that Michelle, who probably had her ear pressed against it, would fall over. "What else does Michelle say?"

Tony followed him out. "That you sent flowers to someone name Evangeline McBride."

Sam stared at him in disbelief. "How does she know that?"

Tony shrugged. "She and the florist are second cousins."

"I should have stayed in Chicago."

Michelle, his loyal secretary and the department's efficient dispatcher, pretended to file papers when he rounded the corner.

"Cousins, huh?" He arched an eyebrow as he strode past.

"You weren't supposed to tell him!" She pouted at Tony, who winked at her.

"I'll be back. I'm going to check out the suspicious truck on Mrs. Mattson's street and then I'm going to stop home for a few minutes." Sam took his sunglasses out of his pocket and shook them open before reaching the door.

"Oh, that's right," Michelle called after him. "My mother's aunt Thelma reupholsters furniture and she said you can drop the recliner off anytime this weekend."

"Thanks." He planned to make his brother pay for the damages Rocky had inflicted on his favorite chair. In a moment of what Sam could only claim as temporary insanity, he'd offered to take care of Rocky until Dan came home. Rachel had changed her mind about having a dog in the house but the hours she and Faith spent with Dan at the rehab center weren't conducive to training an active puppy.

Neither were his, but he'd offered anyway.

Rocky missed his littermates and didn't like being cooped up all day, so he'd taken out his frustration on Sam's recliner. And a pair of boots. And the leg of a coffee table.

"I'll be back later. Don't call me unless it's an absolute emergency."

"Absolute emergency. Got it."

Sam glanced over his shoulder and saw Michelle curtsey and Tony salute.

Comedians. Both of them.

Sam rolled his eyes but tamped down the laughter welling up inside him. The price he paid for being the chief of police in a small town. And he loved it.

If only he could convince Evie that she would love it, too.

Chapter Twenty-One

"You knew about this, Lord," Evie said out loud as she read the bright blue, wave-shaped sign that greeted visitors at the city limits.

Summer Harbor.

Of *course* it was on the water. The little town Sam had promised to protect and serve curled around a sparkling, diamond-shaped bay like a contented tabby cat.

Evie tapped the brake as the speed limit sign suddenly took a radical drop from 55 mph to 25 mph. She didn't want to get picked up for exceeding the speed limit!

She refused to let herself be charmed by the tidy, old-fashioned main street with its brass light poles and wrought-iron benches. Or by the planters, overflowing with pink and white petunias, strategically placed at every corner. She could see the top of an old stone lighthouse jutting from the top of a hill that overlooked Lake Michigan.

There was no sense admiring a town she might only be visiting for fifteen minutes. Depending on how Sam reacted to her unexpected—and unannounced—arrival.

In a town of five thousand people, it didn't take Evie long to locate the police department. One squad car was parked in front of the brick building with the engine running.

Evie's heart jumped.

Okay, God. I'm taking a risk here. Don't leave me.

She pushed open the door and the dispatcher, a young woman with spiky blond hair and jewel-studded glasses perched on her nose, smiled at her from behind the Plexiglas window. When she stood up and waddled over, Evie was surprised to see she was *very* pregnant. "Can I help you?"

"I'm looking for Sam Cutter."

"He's not here right now," the dispatcher said. "Would you like to speak with Officer Faller?"

"No, thank you." Evie gnawed on her lower lip as she tried to determine what to do next. Wait? Go back home?

The second choice was tempting, but she'd driven almost half the day to see Sam.

As she waffled, the door opened behind her and Evie's knees turned to jelly.

"Evangeline McBride?"

Evie turned toward the unfamiliar voice and saw

a man in uniform standing there, looking just as surprised as she was.

"Yes?"

Behind the glass, the dispatcher gasped. "You're Evangeline McBride?"

Evie's gaze cautiously slid from one to the other. How did they know who she was? Was it possible Sam had *talked* about her? To the people he worked with? A flutter of wild hope took wing in her heart.

"I ran your license plate before I came in," the officer said cheerfully. "I'm Officer Faller, by the way."

"And I'm Michelle Loomis." The dispatcher grinned.

"It's nice to meet you both," Evie stammered.

"I told her Chief's not here." Michelle gave Tony a meaningful look.

"I can come back—" If she didn't lose her nerve.

"No!" Their combined voices drowned out her weak suggestion.

"He won't be gone long. Why don't you wait in his office." Officer Faller stepped in front of the door, effectively blocking her path.

Evie eased around him. "No. Thank you. Really. I'll come back…later."

Michelle and Tony exchanged skeptical looks.

"He said we should call him if it's an absolute emergency," Tony mused.

Michelle ignored Evie's strangled protest and nodded thoughtfully. "If she is Evangeline McBride,

I think she definitely falls into the category of an absolute emergency."

Evie tried not to overthink Michelle's remark as the dispatcher scrawled something on a piece of paper and pushed it toward her through the narrow slot in the divider. "Here you go, honey. But don't tell him where you got it. I happen to like my job."

Rocky greeted Sam at the door, a tattered baseball cap clamped in his jaws.

"Found a new hat, huh, boy?" Sam held the door open and Rocky charged past him, on a mission to find the perfect spot to bury the hat. Just like he had the coffee table leg.

The July sunshine beat down on him and Sam loosened his tie as he followed Rocky's crooked trail down the beach.

The remnants of an elaborate sand castle caught his attention, and he immediately thought about Evie.

When *didn't* he think about Evie?

Given the short time they'd known each other, Sam was amazed at how many things reminded him of her. When he looked out his living room window at the water, he remembered the afternoon on the *Natalie*. And her blue eyes. If he saw a woman on the street with a hair color similar to Evie's, his heart rate spiked in response.

Rocky let out a sharp bark and Sam lifted one hand to shade his eyes against the sun. The woman walking toward him on the beach wore a large straw hat. Just like Evie's.

There you go again.

Sam whistled but Rocky ignored him and made a mad dash for the woman, his stubby legs churning up sand like the wheels of a dune buggy.

"He's friendly," Sam shouted across the distance, hoping she wouldn't think his crazy dog was about to attack her.

"I know."

The laughter in the voice—even the voice itself—sounded like Evie. The heat was getting to him. No doubt about it.

As the woman reached down to pet Rocky, he saw the gigantic purse slung over her shoulder.

Somehow, Sam's feet kept moving. Even though everything inside had frozen solid.

"I can't believe he's gotten so big." The straw hat listed to one side and Sam caught a glimpse of sunset-red hair. And a straight little nose dotted with freckles.

Twelve of them.

He couldn't believe Evie was standing three feet away. Almost within reach. Sam blinked, just to make sure she wasn't a hallucination.

"What are you doing here?" He hadn't expected to see her, not unless circumstances forced them together. Sam had discovered his newfound faith meant trusting God when it came to his relationship with Evie. And that had become his greatest challenge.

As the days slipped by with no contact between them, Sam had started to lose hope that she could accept his career. And not only accept it, but support it.

Sam knew God was the only one who could wipe away the last barrier standing between him and Evie. But she had to *let* Him. Accepting that had been tough for Sam, especially when he wanted to crash through those barriers himself and *make* Evie see they were meant to have a future together. Sam had come to the realization that trusting God took guts, a lot more than trying to do things on his own!

"They got the permits." Evie smiled uncertainly. "Yesterday."

She'd driven all the way to Summer Harbor to tell him about the *Noble?*

"That's great. Sophie will be happy." He'd talked to Jacob the night before, but somehow his father had failed to mention the latest news. Maybe because they'd sent Evie to deliver it in person?

Why?

Sam was afraid to hope.

"The local news interviewed Sophie and our dads last night. They're celebrities now. Even a national network called to find out what was going on."

"Great." Sam tried to muster some enthusiasm. He was glad the months of research had yielded some results, but he found himself wishing Evie would have come to Summer Harbor for another reason other than playing messenger. "Have you been in Cooper's Landing the whole time?"

"I went home last week."

"How's the garden?" Sam winced. Okay, there'd been a grain of sarcasm in the question, but seeing Evie again had knocked him off center.

He stuffed his hands in his pockets, not sure how much longer he could hold out before taking her into his arms.

He wasn't making this easy for her. But then, this was a Sam that Evie didn't recognize. He'd had his hair cut since the last time she'd seen him and the five-o'clock stubble that shadowed his lean jawline was gone. He'd traded in his blue jeans and faded T-shirt for charcoal-gray Dockers and a crisp white shirt, paired with a conservative tie. The pockets displayed an assortment of pins. And his badge.

Sam didn't look like a windblown sailor anymore. He looked like a cop.

And she fell in love with him all over again.

From the minute she'd followed the path down to the beach and saw Sam walking by the water, she wondered why she'd let so much time go by. And why she'd let her fears control her future.

She'd put that control right where it had always been—in God's faithful hands. And she planned to leave it there.

Now she just had to convince Sam. If she hadn't waited too long already.

"It's a pretty town." Small talk. So maybe she wasn't as brave as she hoped to be!

"It's on the water," Sam pointed out.

Evie ignored the slight challenge in his tone. "I think it's prettier than Cooper's Landing, with the marina and the lighthouse."

"You like the lighthouse?"

Evie nodded.

"Come on. I'll show it to you."

Evie blinked. Had she imagined Sam's hint of a smile? "Really? I'd like that." She'd like anything that kept him with her.

Sam whistled for Rocky and this time the puppy bounded over and followed them up the beach. The stone lighthouse was smaller than others Evie had seen, but still quaint and well preserved. Probably due to being the target project of a local historical society.

Sam shocked her by following the uneven flagstone path right to the front door.

"You can go inside?" Evie frowned. "Is it open to tourists?"

Instead of answering, Sam turned the handle and stepped to one side.

"Are you sure?" She hesitated. "Don't we need permission?"

"After you." Now Sam did smile. And she would have followed him anywhere.

Evie decided the town must own the lighthouse and, as chief of police, Sam had permission to show it to visitors.

Rocky galloped over to them, his tail wagging proudly as he deposited a shoe at Evie's feet.

"Oh, no, you don't," Sam growled. "I happen to like that pair."

While he wrestled for control of the shoe, Evie turned in a slow circle and scanned the interior. Comfortable furnishings reflected a rustic, nautical theme and Evie realized the lighthouse had been converted into someone's...home. The truth suddenly dawned on her.

"You live in a lighthouse."

God, you knew about this, too! Are there any more surprises?

She hoped so. She was beginning to enjoy them.

"I bought it already fixed up. Over the years it's been a gift shop and an artist's studio, but the last owner put it up for sale within days after the police and fire commission hired me." Sam shrugged. "I couldn't resist."

Evie walked over to the circular staircase that wound up to the second floor.

"Do you want to take a look?"

"I don't like heights." A reluctant confession. Sam was going to think she was still afraid of her own shadow.

"Neither do I," Sam surprised her by saying. "But the view is worth it."

His cell phone rang and he flipped it open. "Excuse me, Evie. I have to take this."

So formal. So professional. When had Sam become the cautious one? And what was she going to have to do to prove to him that her perspective had changed?

"Of course." *I guess I've taken up enough of your time.*

While Sam stepped into the next room, Evie walked blindly outside into the sunshine.

Had she been wrong about Sam's feelings? Had she read too much into his unexpected kiss that day at the beach? Maybe he'd realized he didn't want to pursue a relationship with someone he thought couldn't accept his career.

Rocky followed her and made a beeline toward the lacey waves lapping against the shore. Without thinking, Evie peeled off her shoes and dropped them in the sand as she followed him into the shallow water.

He fished a wet stick of driftwood out of the surf and danced up to her. Evie laughed and tossed it into the water, unable to avoid getting splashed as he went after it.

They played the game for several minutes before Evie felt Sam's presence. She turned around and there he was, right behind her. Her shoes in his hand.

The warmth in his eyes took her breath away. And gave her the courage she needed.

"I'm sorry, Sam. I should've told you how I felt about you but I was scared and—" Evie decided words weren't enough this time. She stood on her tiptoes and reached up to frame his face with her hands. And kissed him.

Her shoes hit the sand with a thud as Sam drew her into his arms and looked down at her.

"Barefoot, Evangeline?" he murmured. "That's a little…adventurous, don't you think?"

She smiled up at him. "What can I say? I'm my mother's daughter. Do you think you can live with that?"

"I'm looking forward to it," Sam whispered in her ear. "For a very long time."

Epilogue

"Okay, Dad. Why did you call us all here? Did you find the treasure or not?"

Evie suppressed a smile. Leave it to Caitlin to cut to the heart of the matter. Several days before, everyone in the Cutter and McBride families had answered a mysterious summons to come to Cooper's Landing. E-mails flew back and forth but no one knew what was going on. When Evie called her dad to try to pry some information from him, all he told her was to pack her bag for the weekend.

So she had. And she'd picked up Sam along the way.

By mid-afternoon on Saturday, Sophie's backyard was crowded with people. Caitlin and Meghan had managed to get the weekend off, although Evie had a hunch their quick response had more to do with wanting to meet Sam than to find out what, if anything, had been discovered in Lake Superior!

Tyson was a quiet presence but Evie noticed Jacob was careful to include Sophie's son in the conversations. According to Patrick, Tyson had joined a support group for people with addictions. He still shied away from attending church services with Sophie, but he'd met Pastor Wallis several times for breakfast.

And it was good to see Faith again, too. And to finally meet Dan and Rachel.

Evie felt an immediate connection with Sam's twin brother and his wife. To her embarrassment, both Dan and Rachel made a point of seeking her out and thanking her again for tutoring Faith. When Evie tried to downplay her role, Rachel met her gaze evenly and told her it wasn't only the tutoring sessions that had put their daughter on the right track. The piece of beach glass on the table next to her bed proved it. When Faith had returned to Chicago with Sam and Jacob, she'd told her father about Evie's prayer asking God to bring something good out of the accident. And, Rachel assured Evie, He had.

It wasn't the only good thing God had done, Evie thought as she felt the warmth of Sam's fingers laced through hers. When Sam had time off, they'd been spending it together. Sometimes he drove to Brookfield to see her, and other times she made the trip to Summer Harbor. Each time she visited, it got harder to say goodbye. Not only to Summer Harbor, but to Sam. Once upon a time, she could never have imagined herself with a police officer. Now she couldn't imagine life without him.

"I agree with Caitlin," Dan said with a grin. "Not that we don't appreciate all this wonderful food you've provided, but we want some answers now."

Sam's fingers tightened and Evie gave him a reassuring squeeze. She knew what he was thinking. Dan was walking now with the use of canes, but the doctor was optimistic he could retire them in time for Faith's basketball season.

Jacob's laugh drew Evie's attention back to the moment. "We can all go in the house and then Sophie can tell you. She's the one who started this whole thing."

Everyone squeezed into Sophie's tiny living room and Sophie set a plain brown folder down on the coffee table. "While the dive team was looking for the *Noble*, Patrick and I kept looking for more information about my great-grandfather Matthew. A few days ago, a retired pastor sent me something.

"The Church on the Hill was the first church in Cooper's Landing, started in the late 1800s by a circuit preacher at the request of the settlers here. It closed its doors about twenty-five years ago, but the original building is still there and so is the cemetery. The records of all the births and deaths were turned over to the local historical society. The pastor I contacted is a member of that society and he was very interested in Matthew's story. The name *Graham* caught his attention and he did some detective work for me."

Sophie hesitated and everyone in the room was silent, waiting for her to continue. Instead, Sophie removed a photograph from the folder on the table.

Evie looked closer and saw an image of an old headstone, pitted and scarred by the elements.

D. C. Graham
Beloved Wife
Born January 10, 1870
Died October 23, 1890

Sam frowned. "Another relative of yours, Sophie?"

"In a matter of speaking." Sophie's eyes misted over. "This headstone is in a section of the cemetery designated to remember people who died but weren't able to be buried. People who perished in blizzards and were never found. Or people who… drowned."

Judging from the confused expressions on the faces gathered around her, Evie knew she wasn't the only one having a hard time following Sophie.

"We think D.C. stands for Dale Carrington," Sophie explained softly. "While I researched our genealogy, I didn't find anyone in my family with those initials."

"But the last name is Graham. And it says beloved wife," Meghan said.

"Exactly." Patrick winked at his middle daughter.

Evie stared at Sophie and Patrick in amazement. "You think Matthew and Lady Dale were *married?*"

"We had a difficult time believing it, too," Sophie said. "But when we saw this photo, everything fell into place. It explains why Matthew had Lady Dale's family ring in his possession when he was rescued. He hadn't stolen it, she'd *given* it to him. According to relatives, Matthew was a changed man after the ship went down. Bitter. Burdened by guilt. But now I believe the guilt wasn't because he'd stolen Lady Dale's dowry—it was because he hadn't been able to save her."

"But wasn't she engaged to that lumber baron's son?" Rachel asked.

"Yes, but Matthew and Lady Dale would have spent a lot of time together, not only at her family estate in England but also on the journey over," Sophie said. "Stranger things have happened. The Lawrence family had a lot of money but lacked respectability. The Carrington family was just the opposite—that's probably why the marriage was arranged. It's possible Matthew befriended Lady Dale and offered her a way to avoid a marriage with a man described as selfish and hot tempered. Or they were simply two young people who fell in love. Whatever the reason, the ship's captain had the authority to perform a wedding ceremony on board the *Noble.*"

"But if they got married, why didn't Matthew tell anyone? It would have saved his reputation," Caitlin asked, clearly skeptical.

"The proof went down with the ship," Patrick said. "The Lawrence family had a lot of influence in this area. Who'd believe a titled lady would give up everything for a lumberjack?"

Meghan gave the barest of smiles. "I would. God knows what He's doing when He brings two people together."

Sophie smiled up at Jacob and he turned red. "Yes. Well. I guess I can go along with that."

Evie felt the warmth of Sam's gaze. "So can I."

"So there's no treasure?" Tyson sounded disappointed. "All that work was for nothing?"

"The treasure is right here." Sophie tapped the photo with the tip of her finger. "For me, it was always about finding the truth."

"I suppose." Tyson sighed.

Patrick's lips twitched. "Maybe you should show him the other photo."

Sophie took something else out of the folder and slid it toward Tyson. "We turned these over to the underwater salvage and preserve committee yesterday. They were pretty excited, to say the least."

Tyson looked dazed. "Gold coins? There has to be at least—"

"Fifty of them," Patrick finished.

"Where—"

"Aw, that's up to the committee to decide." Jacob cleared his throat. "Doesn't matter to me what happens to them. Or even that we cleared Matthew's name. I think we found something a whole lot more valuable than a bunch of old coins."

Sam's eyes glistened as he brushed his lips against Evie's hair. "So do I."

"Did you see those two?" Jacob chuckled. "Who would have guessed?"

Patrick joined him at the window and saw Evie and Sam standing together in the moonlight, deep in conversation.

"We have a lot to be thankful for, my friend."

Jacob blew out a gusty sigh. "Isn't that the truth? But you know something, now that we found the *Noble,* I am going to miss the excitement."

"Mmm." Patrick smiled slowly. "Maybe we don't have to miss it yet."

"What do you mean?"

"After we made the six-o'clock news last week, I got a call from someone."

"About what?"

"Let's just say it may involve another…fishing trip."

Jacob grinned. "Count me in. Partner."

* * * * *

Dear Reader,

Many stories are born from the simple question "What if?" What if a young woman who doesn't like to take risks is suddenly pushed into an adventure? And what if the things she views as flaws, or weaknesses, in her personality turn out to be strengths when they're put to the test?

I love that God created each of us with unique personalities. And I love that He puts us in situations guaranteed to stretch us beyond our abilities—so we learn to trust Him more.

I hope you enjoyed teaming up with Sam and Evie in the romantic adventure, *A Treasure Worth Keeping*. And be sure to watch for Meghan's story—we're not done with the McBride family yet!

Blessings,

Kathryn Springer

QUESTIONS FOR DISCUSSION

1. What is your first impression of Evie? Does it change over the course of the book? Why?

2. How did Evie's and Sam's childhoods differ? How did Jacob Cutter, Sam's father, influence Sam's faith (or lack of it)? How did Sam's childhood differ from the way Patrick raised his daughters? Think about the legacy of faith in your own family as you were growing up. How would you describe it?

3. Dan's injury caused Sam to question what he believed. Has anything happened in a similar situation in your own life? Describe what happened and how it changed your perspective.

4. Evie was a believer, but there was an area in her life where she struggled with totally putting her trust in God. What was it? What did it stem from?

5. When did Sam's opinion of Evie begin to change? Why?

6. What is your favorite scene in the book? Why?

7. Evie compares herself to her sisters and thinks she doesn't measure up to them. What is the

danger in comparing ourselves to other women? Why do you think we tend to do this?

8. Have you ever researched your family history? Do you think it's important? Why or why not?

9. In what way did losing her mother affect the way Evie lived her life? How did it impact her relationships? Why do you think that Evie had to be the one to reach out to Sam at the end of the book?

10. What would you say is your greatest "treasure"? Why?

HEARTWARMING INSPIRATIONAL ROMANCE

Contemporary,
inspirational romances
with Christian characters
facing the challenges
of life and love
in today's world.

**NOW AVAILABLE IN REGULAR
AND LARGER-PRINT FORMATS.**

Steeple
Hill®

For exciting stories that reflect traditional values,
visit:
www.SteepleHill.com

LIGEN07R

Love Inspired®
SUSPENSE
RIVETING INSPIRATIONAL ROMANCE

Watch for our new series of
edge-of-your-seat suspense novels.
These contemporary tales
of intrigue and romance
feature Christian characters
facing challenges to their faith...
and their lives!

Steeple
Hill®

Visit:
www.SteepleHill.com